DEBATED

IMMIGRATION

AMERICAN ISSUES

DEBATED

IMMIGRATION

Herbert M. Levine

RSVP®

**RAINTREE
STECK-VAUGHN**
P U B L I S H E R S
The Steck-Vaughn Company

Austin, Texas

For Glen Jeansonne

Published by Raintree Steck-Vaughn Publishers, an imprint of Steck-Vaughn Company
Publishing Director: Walter Kossmann
Graphic Design & Project Management: Gino Coverty
Editors: Kathy DeVico, Shirley Shalit
Photo Editor: Margie Foster
Electronic Production: Gino Coverty

Library of Congress Cataloging-in-Publication Data
Levine, Herbert M.
Immigration / Herbert M. Levine.
p. cm.—(American issues debated)
Includes bibliographical references and index.
Summary: Presents information on all sides of the immigration issues of today, discussing illegal immigration, immigration and the economy, assimilation, and other aspects.
ISBN 0-8172-4353-4
1. United States--Emigration and immigration--Government policy--Juvenile literature. 2. United States--Emigration and immigration--Juvenile literature.
[1. United States--Emigration and immigration.]   I. Title.   II. Series.
JV6483.L49   1998
304.873--dc21   97-13238
                                  CIP
                                  AC

Printed and bound in the United States
1 2 3 4 5 6 7 8 9 0 LB 01 00 99 98 97

Photograph Acknowledgments
Cover: © PhotoDisc; pp. 10, 13 Corbis-Bettmann; p. 14 © Philip Gould/Corbis; p. 18 Corbis-Bettmann; p. 25 The Granger Collection; p. 28 G. D. Hackett/Archive Photos; pp. 31, 33, 40 UPI/Corbis-Bettman; p. 43 © A. Ramey/Stock Boston; p. 51 © Reuters/Peter Morgan/Archive Photos; p. 54 © Michael V. Guthrie/Archive Photos; p. 62 © Department of Health and Human Services; p. 68 © Joe Rodriguez/ Black Star; p. 71 Erich Hartmann/Magnum Photos; p. 73 © Michael Grecco/Stock Boston; p. 74 © Rob Nelson/Black Star; p. 80 © Reuters/Sam Mircovich/Archive Photos; p. 89 © A. Ramey/Stock Boston; p. 92 © Stephen Ferry/Gamma Liason; p. 94 © M. Grecco/Stock Boston; p. 106 © Rene Burri/Magnum Photos; p. 112 © Dirck Halstead/Gamma Liaison.

CONTENTS

Chapter 1
INTRODUCTION: A NATION OF IMMIGRANTS

Sailing past the Statue of Liberty with her torch held skyward, millions of newcomers to the United States arrived by ship in New York Harbor in the early 1900s. These were immigrants—people who come to a country to take up permanent residence. Although they could not see it from the ship, some of them knew that at the base of the statue were the engraved words of the American poet Emma Lazarus that welcomed them:

> Give me your tired, your poor,
> Your huddled masses yearning to breathe free,
> The wretched refuse of your teeming shore.
> Send these, the homeless, tempest-tost to me,
> I lift my lamp beside the golden door!

Most of the immigrants on these ships went ashore at Ellis Island, just off Manhattan, where immigration officials determined whether the passengers carried the necessary documents and met financial, health, and other requirements that would allow them to speed to their points of destination in the United States. In the early 1900s, most of the newcomers were from eastern and southern Europe—particularly Russia, Poland, Greece, and Italy. Today, immigrants continue to arrive in the United States each day. They are no longer likely to pass by the Statue of Liberty, because New York is not now the major entry point for immigrants. They are no longer likely to arrive by ship either, because most of them—at least, those who enter legally—arrive by airplane. Their point of entry is likely to be Los Angeles International Airport, and most of them come from Asia or Latin America.

The Immigrants

In the 20th century as in the past, the United States remains a nation of immigrants. It is built on the migrations of peoples from many regions of the world with differences in religious faiths, languages, and racial features. The earliest immigrants to what became North America arrived at some time between 30,000 B.C. and 13,000 B.C. They came from Asia by moving from Siberia, crossing the land that is now covered by the Bering Sea, and arriving in Alaska. Gradually, over a period of thousands of years, they proceeded down the Pacific coast to a warmer climate. They hunted and fished but took up agriculture around the beginning of the first century A.D. In the next 1,500 years, they constructed irrigation projects and grew plants, such as corn, potatoes, and tobacco. By the early 16th century, fewer than one million Native Americans (or Indians, as Christopher Columbus had misnamed them) lived in what is now the United States.

Europeans were early travelers to North America, although the exact date of their arrival is unknown. Legend has it that an Irish monk, Saint Brendan, reported discovering islands far out in the Atlantic in the 5th century. The Vikings, who were from Scandinavia, landed in Newfoundland and named it Vinland around the year 1000. But the Vikings established no permanent settlements.

Europeans began to leave the Old World (Europe) and settle in the New World (the Western Hemisphere) in the 16th century as explorers discovered new lands. The territory that became the United States contained people from many ethnic groups (people who share common features, such as race, language, and culture) even before the United States declared its independence from Great Britain in 1776. Great Britain controlled and established settlements in North America east of the Alleghenies and between Florida and Canada by the middle of the 18th century. Spain held territory in the South—Florida, Texas, New Mexico, and California. The French built settlements along the Mississippi and Ohio River valleys. Germans settled in Pennsylvania, Dutch in the Hudson Valley of New York, and Swedes in Delaware. In 1755, the Acadians, who were French Catholics, went into exile to Louisiana from Nova Scotia and New Brunswick when those Canadian territories came under British rule. Former President John F. Kennedy observed in *A Nation of Immigrants*: "When Britain conquered Nieuw Amsterdam [New York] in 1664, it offered citizenship to immigrants of eighteen different nationalities."

Immigration grew once the American people gained independence from Great Britain in 1783. At times, the number of people who voluntarily immigrated was small, but at other times the number grew large within a relatively short period of time. And the places from which immigrants came varied over time. Historians speak of three waves of immigration to the United States before World War I. The first wave of five million people came between 1815 and 1860. They were mostly from Great Britain, Germany, Scandinavia, Switzerland, and Holland. The second wave of ten million people came between 1860 and 1890 and were from the same general areas as the first wave. The third wave of 15 million people came between 1890 and 1914 and were mostly from Austria-Hungary, Italy, Russia, Greece, Romania, and Turkey. About 300,000 Chinese crossed the Pacific to the United States between 1850 and 1882.

A major shift in the background of immigrants occurred in the 1960s. Between 1820 and 1960, 85 percent of immigrants to the United States came from Europe, 13 percent from Western Hemisphere countries, and 3 percent from Asia. But the pattern changed dramatically to one in which large numbers of immigrants came from the Third World (the poorer, developing nations mostly in Africa, Asia, and Latin America). As historian Maldwyn Allen Jones notes: "By the 1980's, Europe was contributing barely 10 per cent of the total, whereas the Americas were sending 45 per cent and Asia an additional 41 per cent."

Why Immigrants Came

People came to America for different reasons. Scholars use the terms push and pull to describe the factors that convinced immigrants to make the trip. "Push" refers to the forces in the country of origin that encourage or drive people to leave. "Pull" refers to the opportunities in the chosen land that encourage immigrants to leave their home country.

"Push" forces have come in part from great economic suffering, such as the Irish potato famine from 1845 to 1849, in which a million Irish died of starvation. To survive, many Irish people had no choice other than to leave their homeland; and 1,600,000 fled to the United States. According to economist Thomas Sowell: "Altogether, about a third of the total population of Ireland disappeared in a few years in the mid-1840s. By 1914, the population of Ireland was one-half of what it had been in the 1840s." Another group that left largely for "push" reasons were the Jews of Russia. They came to America in the 1880s because the Russian government encouraged violent acts against them. Jews were forced to live only in the Pale of Settlement, a territory between the Baltic Sea and the Black Sea. From time to time, there were pogroms—government-encouraged massacres of Jews and destruction of their property and religious institutions. So grim was life for Jews that by 1914, one-third of all the Jews in Russia and eastern Europe emigrated (left their country to live in another country), most to the United States.

Political exiles (people who leave their country either voluntarily or involuntarily) came to America in search of freedom. Exiles came from France because of the French Revolution of 1789, from Ireland after the disturbances of 1798, 1803, and 1848, and from Germany with the failure of a revolution in 1848. In recent years,

This engraving depicts crowds at the Irish Emigrant Office in New York City, at the start of the Irish potato famine in 1845.

exiles fled Cuba after 1959 when Fidel Castro established a Communist government there.

"Pull" factors include such matters as greater economic opportunity and religious and political freedom that would not be available to people in their homelands. The prospect of cheap land encouraged European farmers to migrate (move). Some foreigners migrated because they wanted to establish their own churches.

Although the reasons for leaving home countries differed among immigrant groups and even within immigrant groups, some factors were more important than others. Historian Roger Daniels contends that for "most immigrants...economic betterment was the major motivating force."

Whether because of push or pull reasons, most immigrants came of their own free will. The only people to be brought here against their will were African Americans who came over from Africa as slaves, most of them to work in tobacco or cotton fields. So crowded and unsafe were the slave ships that many slaves died during the sea journey across the Atlantic.

Although many immigrants came to the United States voluntarily and legally, a large number did not stay. Some left their countries because they only intended to come for a short period of time and return as soon as they made enough money to take back. Many Chinese and Italian immigrants fell into this category, for example. Chinese immigrants in the 19th century were mostly men, who left their families behind because they expected to join them in China in a few years. Also, many people from varied ethnic groups returned to their homeland because they found life in America to be too challenging for them to make a living or because they found that the difficulties of learning English or adapting to an unfamiliar—and sometimes hostile—environment to be harsh. According to historian Rowland Berthoff, 55 percent as many English people returned home as left for the United States between 1895 and 1918. And ethnic scholar Ronald Takaki observes that 55 percent of the 200,000 Japanese who went to Hawaii between 1886 and 1924 returned to Japan.

The Journey and Life of Immigrants
For many immigrants, the trip to the United States in the early 19th century was a difficult or even terrible event. The long journey started inland in Europe, requiring long walks to the seaports and waiting for ships. Sailing vessels meant long journeys. In the era of sailing ships, the average trip from Liverpool, England, to New York, took 40 days. Eight to 12 weeks was the normal range in time for transatlantic crossings. In the days of sailing ships, immigrants came in the hold (the lower, interior part) of cargo ships. In the early 19th century, immigrants who made this trip were subject to diseases from crowded conditions. Many suffered from seasickness as their ships pitched and rolled easily. According to some accounts, one in ten people did not survive the sailing ship journey across the Atlantic.

Improvements in transportation technology meant not only that large numbers of people could come to the United States, but also they could settle in areas throughout the country. After 1820 these improvements were marked by steam power for ships across the Atlantic. The construction of turnpikes, canals, and railroads across the country between 1815 and 1860 revolutionized transportation on land and water within the United States. By 1860, railroads and steamboats had connected the regions of the nation.

Some immigrants settled in the nearest place they could reach. Many moved to areas where members of their fellow racial, religious, or ethnic group were living. The nearest place for early European settlers was along the mid- and north-Atlantic seaboard. The nearest places for Asians were California and the Pacific states, and for Mexicans California and the southwestern states. The immigrants also settled in places where they could find work, such as in the Midwest, as industrial development required the services of laborers. The earliest wave of immigrants settled in seaports where the immigrants usually arrived: Boston, Philadelphia, Baltimore, New Orleans, and New York. But with the opening up of the continent, immigrants settled in places where rail and river traffic met, such as Cleveland, Chicago, Pittsburgh, and St. Louis.

The nation welcomed immigrants and placed few barriers to their arrival—at least not until late in the 19th century. With a vast continent to develop, the United States needed unskilled workers to build canals, roads, and railroads. A booming economy furnished opportunities for immigrants to work in factories and on farms. At first, however, the factories did not welcome immigrants because much of the work required skilled labor, which many immigrants lacked. But with the invention of new technologies, immigrants could be employed in such industries as the manufacturing of clothing and furniture. And a mineral-rich nation required the services of unskilled immigrant labor in mining, such as in the coal and oil fields.

Many who arrived in the United States experienced difficult economic times. In the 17th and 18th centuries, a principal means for

Crowded living conditions were common in American cities during the late 19th and early 20th centuries.

coming to America was as indentured servants. These were men and women who in return for payment of their passage agreed to work from four to seven years for the employers to whom they were assigned. After the work obligation was fulfilled, the person was free to move on. In 17th-century Virginia, 75 percent of the immigrants came as indentured servants.

In the 19th and early 20th centuries, many immigrants in the cities lived crowded into tenements (inexpensive, poor quality apartments that were small and lacked good sanitary conditions). It is not surprising that disease took a heavy toll in health and life of the people who lived in such conditions.

The Contributions of Immigrants to American Society

Every group who came to America can rightly claim to have made a contribution to the nation's achievements. Some notable examples include Andrew Carnegie, the industrialist and philanthropist, who was from Scotland. Thomas Paine, an Englishman, wrote *Common Sense*, an important pamphlet published in 1776 that called for the independence of the American colonies from Great Britain.

The German-born John Jacob Astor built the fur industry. Pierre Samuel Du Pont de Nemours, an immigrant from France, established a powder works company in Wilmington, Delaware, in 1802, which eventually became a leading chemical and munitions industry. Enrico Fermi, an Italian immigrant, was a top contributor to the nation's leadership in atomic research. Walter Knudsen from Denmark was a major figure in the automobile industry. Alexander Hamilton, George Washington's first secretary of the treasury, was born in the West Indies. Albert Gallatin, a Swiss, was secretary of the treasury in the administration of President Thomas Jefferson.

Henry Kissinger, a German immigrant, played a crucial role in U.S. foreign policy during the Nixon administration.

Among Americans of German ancestry who made contributions to U.S. national security is Henry Kissinger, who was secretary of state in the administration of Richard Nixon. John Shalikashvili, an immigrant from Poland, was the chairman of the Joint Chiefs of Staff during the presidency of Bill Clinton. A German Jewish immigrant, Levi Strauss, was a peddler. It is he for whom the denim trousers known as Levis are named. I. M. Pei, an American architect born in China, designed many structures, including the East Wing of the National Gallery of Art in Washington, D.C., the Mile High Center in Denver, and the John Hancock Tower in Boston.

Some groups made contributions to particular sectors of American society. African Americans, both as immigrants and descendants of immigrants, have excelled particularly in entertainment and athletics. Irish Americans have been prominent in politics. In the 19th century, the Chinese helped build U.S. railroads. In the 20th century, Asian Americans have been prominent in computer science and engineering. Many East European Jews were in the garment industry. Mexican Americans participated in large numbers in developing America's agriculture. Of course, none of these groups had a monopoly in any field because talent, intelligence, and other ingredients of success are found in every group.

Immigrants, too, have contributed to our language and culture. Germans contributed words, such as "kindergarten," "hamburger," and "delicatessen." The Christmas tree, which is so much a part of American life that every year the President begins the holiday season with a lighted tree in front of the White House, is itself a German tradition. But then again, some things that are associated with a particular ethnic group have their origins in the United States rather than a foreign culture. For example, chow mein and chop suey are American and not Chinese. The hot dog, a kind of sausage served in a long roll, is also an American invention, not German.

The contributions of immigrants to American society are a continuing story. Historian Oscar Handlin summed up the contributions when he wrote: "They [the immigrants] helped settle the continent; they developed the industry of the country; they confirmed the pluralism [the condition in which different ethnic and other groups live at peace in a political community] and freedom of American society; and they made substantial contributions to the transfer of culture from the Old to the New World."

Supporters and Opponents of Immigration

Although at times, the nation's political leaders hail the achievements of immigrants, on other occasions, they have been critical and even hostile toward foreigners who want to be part of the American political community. The American people have really had a love-hate relationship with immigrants. In the 17th century, colonial America needed immigrants, who provided labor and security for the small numbers of Europeans who were already settlers. In general, business groups favored immigrants, particularly during periods of expanding economic development. As indicated above, the nation's industry needed workers to mine coalfields, build railroads, manufacture products, and help farm the land.

In the past and the present, many business leaders understood that an abundance of immigrants would help keep worker supply high and labor costs low. According to Ronald Takaki, speaking of the period after World War I, "Chicanos [Mexican Americans] migrated to midwestern and eastern cities where managers of factories and steel mills recruited them as a strategy to prevent strikes. 'If there are a couple of thousand waiting for a job, those who are working won't strike.'" Some businesses today even prefer to hire illegal immigrants because they are not likely to complain about wages that are regarded as low by legal U.S. workers or about work conditions that are unsafe and in violation of the law. Illegal immigrants are frightened to complain because they fear being reported to immigration officials who will deport (send out of the country by legal means) them.

In general, ethnic groups support the admission of immigrants from their own groups and cultures. Among Hispanic organizations, for example, are the National Council of La Raza (NCLR), the

League of United Latin American Citizens (LULAC), and the Mexican American Legal Defense and Educational Fund (MALDEF). Religious and humanitarian groups often speak for the cause of immigrants, too. Some political groups favor the admission of immigrants who are victims of oppressive political regimes that they oppose. For example, U.S. anticommunists encouraged admitting Hungarians fleeing their country as a result of the Hungarian Revolution of 1956, which was put down by the Soviet Union, a powerful rival of the United States.

Opposition to immigrants has pre-American Revolution roots, indicating that there has always been some anti-immigrant feeling in America. Although the nation welcomed immigrants, at times it had serious criticisms and prejudices against particular groups of people. As early as 1751, Benjamin Franklin wrote a pamphlet, *Observations Concerning the Increase of Mankind,* in which he complained about the Germans: "Why should Pennsylvania, founded by the English, become a Colony of Aliens [foreign-born citizens], who will shortly be so numerous as to Germanize [make German] us instead of our Anglifying [make English] them, and will never adopt our Language or Customs, any more than they can acquire our Complexion[?]" When the Alien and Sedition Acts (laws that lengthened the number of years in which people had to be in the United States before gaining citizenship, allowed the President to expel "dangerous" aliens, and forbade criticism of the government) were passed in the late 18th century, some Americans expressed fear that Roman Catholic immigrants would show loyalty to the pope rather than to their new nation.

With an increase in immigration in the 1840s—particularly of Roman Catholics who lived in eastern cities—some Americans who were native-born favored restricting certain kinds of immigrants from coming into the United States. They also wanted to limit immigrant participation in the American political process. In 1843, an American Republican party was established in New York. Soon other states formed a similar party as the Native American party, which became a national party in 1845. Secret societies favoring restrictions

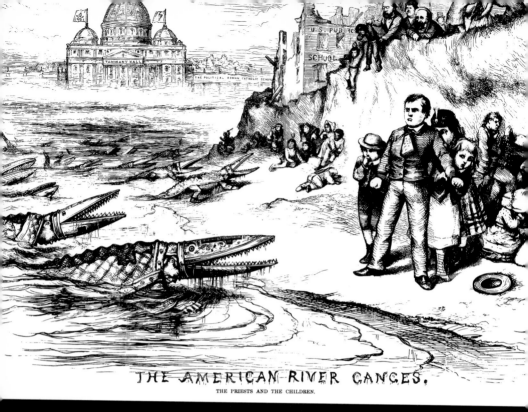

THE AMERICAN RIVER GANGES.
THE PRIESTS AND THE CHILDREN.

This 1871 cartoon reflects the anti-Roman Catholic and anti-immigrant sentiment many native-born Americans shared at the time.

on immigration were set up. Members of these societies agreed not to tell anyone about their organizations. When they were asked about their organizations, they said that they "know nothing" about them, hence they were called "Know Nothings." In 1855, the nativists (those who favor native inhabitants rather than immigrants) changed the name of their party to the American party, which was anti-Roman Catholic and anti-immigrant. The peak of Know Nothing influence occurred in 1855 when the American party elected six governors, dominated several state legislatures, and had many members in Congress. American party influence declined with the defeat of Millard Fillmore, the party's presidential candidate, in 1856. Differences over slavery split the party, and many members joined the newly formed Republican party. The Know Nothings favored assimilating (absorbing into the native culture) the new immigrants. They also wanted to require 21 years of residency (living) in the United States for citizenship and to limit the privileges of voting and holding office. The Civil War reduced opposition to foreigners. As Maldwyn Allen Jones notes: "The many thousands who fought for the Union did so upon terms of equality with the native-born population, and thus lost the sense of inferiority which had dogged them since their coming to America."

At various times in U.S. history, some American workers have objected to immigrants whom they regard as likely to take their jobs or cause their wages to be lowered. In the 1920s, for example, the American Federation of Labor (AFL), a large labor union, tried to restrict the flow of Mexican immigrants. Mexico was not covered by the quota system established in the 1924 immigration law, which sharply cut the immigration flow. (In immigration, a quota system is a system in which a maximum number of persons is permitted to enter the United States from specific countries per year.) An AFL official referred to Mexican employment in American industry as "this great evil."

Some opponents of immigration—or at least the immigration of certain kinds of immigrants (that is, those from a particular race, religion, or ethnic background)—have been particularly effective in influencing immigration legislation. At its most extreme are those who accept the idea that some races are superior to others. Such a view was common in the late 19th and early 20th centuries. It was based on a belief in superior races like Anglo-Saxon (a member of the Germanic peoples—Angles, Saxons, and Jutes—who settled in Britain in the 5th and 6th centuries) and Teutonic (Germanic) peoples. One such group was the Immigration Restriction League. Founded in 1894, it was the most influential pressure group arguing for a fundamental change in American immigration policy. Historian Roger Daniels reports: "According to one of its founders, Prescott F. Hall (1868–1921), the question for Americans to decide was whether they wanted their country 'to be peopled by British, German and Scandinavian stock, historically free, energetic, progressive, or by Slav, Latin and Asiatic races [this latter referred to Jews rather than Chinese or Japanese] historically down-trodden, atavistic [genetically weak] and stagnant.'"

Many who made racial remarks used faulty analysis in assuming that particular ethnic groups had intellectual weaknesses. In this regard, Henry Cabot Lodge, who represented Massachusetts in Congress from 1887 until 1924, supported the Immigration Restriction League and pushed for a literacy test requiring an immigrant to prove his or her ability to read and write. Congress made the literacy test a requirement for a person to immigrate to the United States. (When a family immigrated, however, the wife did not need to be literate if the husband were literate.) But literacy meant capable of reading in any recognized language—English or other. Unexpectedly for those who wanted to restrict immigration, the literacy test had virtually no effect on the number of immigrants. As historian Roger Daniels observes: "During the last full year in which it was the major statutory bar to immigration—July 1920 to June 1921—more than 800,000 immigrants entered the country. About 1.5 percent (13,799 persons) were denied admission on some ground or another, a mere 1,450 of whom were barred by the long-debated test."

The Ku Klux Klan, a well-known racist organization, was active in immigration matters in the 1920s. At that time, it was not only antiblack, anti-Semitic, and anti-Catholic, but it was anti-immigrant, as well. But not all who wish to take ethnic background into consideration in immigration matters are extremists. Some commentators worry that allowing large numbers of immigrants from ethnic backgrounds that differ from the dominant majority to come into the United States can be disruptive of the nation's social stability. These commentators point to the conflict among different ethnic groups in the same country (such as the former Yugoslavia), which has torn apart a political community. Those who have such views fear that the United States will have a similar fate if it is too generous in its immigration policy.

★ ☆ ★ ☆ ★

The immigrant story is central to American history. Many immigrants came to the United States and succeeded beyond their wildest dreams. Others failed and could not find a suitable place in American society. Many returned to their homelands, sometimes happily in keeping with their original intentions, and at other times sadly, reflecting the failure of their dreams for a new life. Because of the different interests and sentiments among Americans about immigrants, the kinds of laws that will be made about immigration in the future will continue to reflect the broad areas of agreement and conflict that the issue of immigration creates.

Chapter 2
IMMIGRATION AND THE LAW

Although Congress has passed laws limiting immigration in general and banning certain groups in particular from immigrating, the United States is still a land of immigrants and has been so for most of its history. No country in the world has been so willing to accept immigrants as the United States—and this willingness existed even before the United States gained its independence from Great Britain. One of the complaints that the men who wrote the Declaration of Independence made against King George III when they declared their independence from Great Britain was: "'He has endeavoured [tried] to prevent the population of these States; for that reason obstructing the Laws for the Naturalization [the granting of full citizenship] of Foreigners; refusing to pass others to encourage their migrations hither, and raising the conditions of new Appropriations [the setting aside for a specific purpose] of Lands."

The Constitution contains little about immigration, but it does distinguish between citizens born in the United States and those who come from foreign countries and are naturalized Americans—that is, made citizens after they immigrate to the United States. The only reference to immigration in the Constitution deals with the slave trade. Article I, Section 9, provides "The Migration or Importation of such Persons as any of the States now existing shall think proper to admit, shall not be prohibited by the Congress prior to the Year one thousand eight hundred and eight, but a Tax or duty may be imposed on such Importation not exceeding ten dollars for each person." Article I, Section 8, gives Congress the power "to establish an uniform Rule of Naturalization." But the section does not specify details. The Constitution makes a distinction between native-born and naturalized citizens in Article I. Section 2 of Article I states that "no Person shall be a Representative [in Congress] who shall not have... been seven Years a Citizen." Section 3 of that article requires that a person becoming a senator be "nine Years a Citizen." And Article II, Section 1 restricts the presidency to "natural born citizens" and persons who were citizens at the time of the adoption of the Constitution.

Congress passed the first naturalization law in 1790. It served to welcome foreigners—at least certain kinds of foreigners, namely "free white persons." Such persons could be naturalized in any American court in a period of as little as two years. The law did not apply to immigrant black people at this time. In the 19th century, when Asians came to the United States, it did not apply to them either. It was not until 1870 when Congress changed the naturalization law that "persons of African descent" could be naturalized. Until 1870, the law in the individual states determined citizenship for non-whites. Native Americans were legally regarded as aliens until 1887 when Congress enacted the Dawes Act (named for Henry Dawes, a U.S. senator from Massachusetts) granting citizenship to Native Americans who accepted a plot of land, lived apart from the tribe, and became part of the dominant white culture. In 1924, Congress extended citizenship to all Native Americans.

In 1795, Congress passed the second naturalization law, increasing the period of residence required to become a citizen to five years. In 1798, Congress passed another naturalization law establishing a 14-year probationary (trial) period before a person could apply for citizenship. The Federalists, the party that controlled Congress at the time, realized that recent immigrants, particularly the Irish, tended to vote for the Republicans, who opposed the Federalists. By setting such a long period for citizenship, the Federalists hoped to stay in power. When the Jeffersonian Republicans came to power, they passed the Naturalization Act of 1801, setting the required residency requirement back to five years—a requirement that continues to the present.

Congress made little effort to restrict immigration until 1875, when it banned the entry of prostitutes and convicts. In 1882, it excluded paupers (extremely poor people), "idiots," and "lunatics." Immigration from China in the 1870s was cause for the Chinese Exclusion Act of 1882, which banned Chinese immigration for ten years. In 1892, the law was extended for another ten years, and in 1902, Congress made it permanent. In 1924, Congress excluded all Asians from immigration. Although the Chinese Exclusion Act stopped Chinese immigration, other laws prevented Chinese already here from becoming naturalized citizens. Laws were passed limiting professional jobs and land ownership to citizens, thus hurting Chinese immigrants. The Chinese could not even testify against whites between 1854 and 1874, so they were denied legal rights when they were robbed or otherwise hurt by white people.

The Japanese, too, experienced discrimination as a result of U.S. laws and policies. They emigrated from Japan in the late 19th century. In the 1880s and 1890s, most Japanese emigrants went to Hawaii and worked as contract laborers on American sugar plantations. When the United States annexed (took control of) Hawaii in 1898, the Japanese who wished to move to the continental United States could do so. For awhile, they did so at the rate of about 10,000 a year.

Many Japanese who came to the continental United States were farmers and businesspeople, and some worked in factories. Japanese Americans mostly settled on the West Coast. California passed the Alien Land Law of 1913. It was an anti-Japanese law that prevented aliens not eligible for citizenship from owning land in that state.

Japan and the United States worked out what became known as the Gentleman's Agreement of 1908, by which Japan limited the

Anti-Chinese advertisements such as this one from around 1886 encouraged discriminatory practices against Chinese immigrants.

number of immigrants to the United States. (A gentleman's agreement is an understanding by which the parties are bound only by their word of honor.) In return, the United States permitted wives of Japanese men who were in the United States to join their husbands and also allowed Japanese parents and their children to be reunited with their families in the United States. It was not until 1943, when the United States and China were allies in World War II, that Chinese were allowed to immigrate to the United States. The ban on Japanese was lifted after World War II.

The Alien Contract Labor Law (1885) prohibited the importation of aliens who were signed to an employment contract before they immigrated to the United States. This law was a response to labor unions that did not want cheap labor to compete with them as well as to reform groups that wished to prevent the exploitation of immigrants.

Those who wished to limit immigration established organizations in the 1890s. They tried to get a literacy test adopted in 1896, 1913, and 1915. They succeeded in gaining congressional approval, but the bills were vetoed by Presidents Grover Cleveland, William Howard Taft, and Woodrow Wilson respectively. Congress was able to pass the literacy test over Wilson's veto in 1917. After World War I, the forces of restriction were strengthened by popular acceptance of isolationism, which is a policy of avoiding entanglements with foreign countries. Some people also had a fear of foreigners with views that were regarded as extremist, such as anarchism and communism. Anarchism is a political philosophy that favors the abolition of government. Communism is a theory in which private property is eliminated, people own the means of production, and goods and services are distributed fairly with the state playing a minimum role in people's lives. In reality, communism is a dictatorial system with the Communist party controlling the government and the economy. Antiradical fears grew in part from the establishment in 1917 of a Communist government in Russia that called for world revolution.

Some of the most restrictive immigration laws were enacted in 1921 and 1924. In 1921, Congress passed temporary legislation that set an annual ceiling at 358,000 immigrants. The major law, however, was the Immigration Act of 1924 (known also as the National Origins Act). The 1924 law:

• Established permanent numerical restrictions upon immigration from all parts of the world (except the Western Hemisphere) under a ceiling of 150,000 per year.

• Limited immigration through a quota system to 2 percent of each nationality as reflected in the 1890 census. This formula heavily favored Great Britain, Ireland, and Germany and reduced the proportion of South and East European immigrants.

• Excluded aliens ineligible for citizenship. (This provision excluded Japanese immigrants. Other legislation had previously excluded Chinese and Asian Indian immigrants.)

No quotas for Canada, Mexico, or any other New World country were established in the 1924 law, however.

The quota system put an end to large-scale immigration to the United States. When the Great Depression, which began in 1929, continued into the 1930s, there was no demand for opening borders. Unemployment took a heavy toll on American workers. President Franklin D. Roosevelt did not open the gates to those fleeing Nazism in the 1930s in part because of the laws and sentiment on immigration. But changing times brought new policies. Labor shortages in World War II led in 1942 to the U.S. government braceros program (from the Spanish word *brazos* or "arms"). Under this program, Mexican agriculture workers were admitted to the United States to work on farms. These workers would return to Mexico after they completed their work contracts. The program continued after the war and ended in 1964.

World War II created a large number of refugees in war-ravaged Europe. An executive order signed by President Harry S Truman in December 1945 allowed more than 40,000 aliens to come to the United States as "displaced persons"—people who were homeless as a result of World War II. In 1948, the Displaced Persons Act provided for the admission of 250,000 displaced persons over a period of two years. In 1950, the law was amended to continue for another two years, and the total was raised to 415,000. Most of those who benefited from the law were ethnic Germans from Eastern Europe and some Baltic peoples. For the most part, Jews did not benefit from this law since few Jews were displaced persons in the Western European refugee camps. The Displaced Persons Act was the first federal law to set refugee policy in contrast to immigration policy. A refugee is a person who flees a country usually out of fear of persecution or war.

After World War II, U.S. immigration policy was heavily influenced by U.S. policy toward the Soviet Union in what became a "cold war." In contrast to a "hot war" involving fighting and other forms of military activity, the cold war involved economic, political, diplomatic, and propaganda attacks by and against each of these strong countries, or superpowers as they were called, because their power was superior to that of other countries. The Internal Security Act of

Many Europeans who lost their homes during World War II arrived by boat at New York Harbor.

1950 barred any person ever connected with a Communist or Fascist movement from immigrating to the United States. (A Fascist is a person who favors dictatorial rule and often makes strong appeals to the overwhelming importance of national unity.) The McCarran-Walter Act of 1952 (named for Patrick McCarran, a U.S. senator from Nevada; and Francis Walter, a congressman from Pennsylvania) ended the total exclusion of certain racial and ethnic groups from naturalization and immigration but preserved the national origin system. The Refugee Act of 1953 authorized the admission of 205,000 persons who were not part of the quota, over a two-and-a-half year period. This refugee law was written for the benefit of those who fled Communist regimes.

One provision of the McCarran-Walter Act allowed the attorney general of the United States, the nation's chief law-enforcement official, to grant temporary admission to aliens for emergency or national-security interests. It was called "parole authority," which is conditional release. Parole authority was used first by President Franklin D. Roosevelt in 1944 to bring in refugees. Presidents used parole authority in the McCarran-Walter Act to bring into the United States refugees from Communist rule, such as Hungarians, Tibetans, Cubans, and Vietnamese. Once the refugees were in the United States, Congress passed laws authorizing their admission. Between 1945 and 1980, more than 2.25 million persons were admitted to the United States as refugees. Other refugees came in as quota and nonquota immigrants.

The Immigration Act of 1965 ended the national origins quota system of 1924. It provided that every country would be allowed the same number of immigrants no matter the size of territory or population. The 1965 law established limits by hemispheres rather than by countries. The annual limits were 170,000 for people from the Eastern Hemisphere and 120,000 for people from the Western Hemisphere. The maximum for any country in the Eastern Hemisphere was 20,000. No similar limit was placed on countries in the Western Hemisphere. The law established a preference system of seven categories to determine which individuals could be included among the 20,000 admitted from an Eastern Hemisphere country. The law made a fundamental change in the immigration system by giving preference to "family reunification." U.S. citizens and resident aliens could bring over spouses, adult children with spouses and children, and brothers and sisters with spouses and children.

In 1976 and 1978, Congress amended the Immigration Act of 1965. The new law merged the separate hemispheric ceilings into a global cap of 290,000 visas (official authorizations to enter a country) and applied the 20,000 ceiling to the Western Hemisphere countries also. No longer did place of birth give a country a preference. The 1976 law also applied the seven-category preference system to applicants from the Western Hemisphere.

The 1965 law resulted in increases of immigrants from Latin America and Asia. Latin American immigrants used family preferences because there were many people of Latin American heritage in the United States. (As mentioned above, people from the Western Hemisphere had not been included in the 1924 law.) Asian immigrants came as a result of occupational preferences in the immigration law that allowed a certain number of professional people and skilled workers to enter the United States. Once settled, they became citizens. Now as American citizens, many Asians brought in members of their families. Also, many Asians came as refugees from the Vietnam War (who in turn brought in family members).

The 1965 law provided for 17,400 refugees a year to be admitted to the United States. But the law had a political aspect to it because it dealt with refugees from Communist countries and those fleeing persecution in the Middle East.

The Refugee Act of 1980 recognized the right of asylum (a place offering protection or safety) for refugees and defined a refugee as "any person who is outside any country of his nationality or in the case of any person having no nationality, is outside of any country in which he has habitually resided, and who is unable or unwilling to return to, and is unwilling to avail [take advantage] himself of the

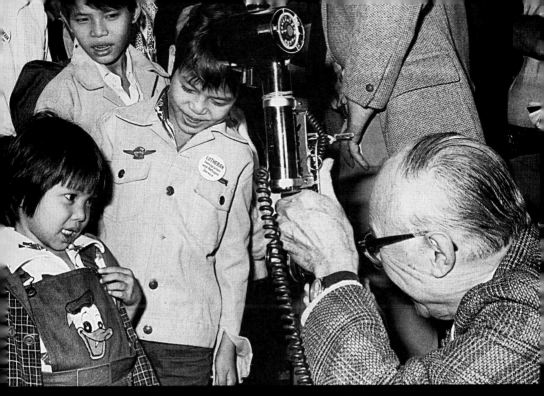

Vietnamese refugees pose for the press after arriving at San Francisco International Airport in 1977.

protection of that country because of persecution, or a well-founded fear of persecution, on account of race, religion, nationality, membership of a particular social group, or political opinion." This definition was the same as the United Nations' definition of refugees and, consequently, was not tied to political objectives, as the old law had been. The law also created a category of "asylees," who were people who were already in the United States either legally or illegally—unlike refugees—but who, like refugees, sought admission to the United States. To stay in the United States, however, asylees had to meet the criteria of refugees. Asylees would leave permanent resident alien status after a one-year waiting period. The 1980 law set a yearly limit of 5,000 asylees. In 1990, the annual ceiling was raised to 10,000 but has risen since then.

The 1980 law removed refugee admissions from the legal immigration system and reduced the legal immigration ceiling to 270,000 people plus immediate relatives. The President, in consultation with Congress, could determine the number of refugees to be admitted. According to economist Vernon M. Briggs, Jr., "The annual admission figures [for refugees] have ranged from a low of 67,000 in 1986 to a high of 217,000 in 1991."

The Immigration Reform and Control Act (IRCA) of 1986 sought some major changes in immigration laws, designed to deal with illegal immigration. It provided for amnesty (an official pardon for breaking a specific law) for illegal immigrants in the United States if they met certain conditions, such as residence, no criminal record, a negative test for AIDS antibodies, a record of financial responsibility, and a knowledge of the English language and U.S. history. If they met the conditions, they could apply for citizenship after five years of residence. More than 2.9 million people gained U.S. citizenship in this manner. The 1986 law also provided for punishment of employers who hired illegal immigrants. But the law had so many loopholes that it had little consequence for stopping the flow of illegal immigrants. (See Chapter 4.)

In the Immigration Act of 1990, another 40,000 to 50,000 visas were set aside for citizens of a country that was regarded as underrepresented since the 1965 law was enacted. The new annual ceiling went up to 700,000 people (including immediate relatives). It reserved about 140,000 visas (20 percent of the 700,000) for individuals (and their dependents) with special job skills and talent. But the 140,000 includes "accompanying family members."

The 1990 law provided for a new category of "investor immigrants" to come in because of their wealth and willingness to invest in the United States. The law also provided for "diversity immigrants" that would admit people from countries that had low rates of immigration since 1965. The diversity immigrant program reserved 40 percent of available visas in this category to immigrants from Ireland. Because the number of applicants was large, a lottery was established to determine who received the visas.

The 1990 law provided for a category known as "non-immigrant workers." This category is for workers who are needed if qualified citizen workers cannot be found to fill a job. These workers are admitted for temporary periods that can be extended.

In 1996, Congress passed two laws that were intended to have a strong impact on immigrants: a welfare reform law and an immigration law. These laws are described in some detail in Chapter 8. The welfare reform law limited welfare benefits for legal immigrants. The immigration law dealt mostly with illegal immigration.

Today, the legal procedure for becoming an immigrant is fairly clear-cut if a person meets the legal tests for immigration. A person applies through the American consulate in his or her country. Once in the United States, an alien applies for permanent residence. If this is granted, the immigrant gets an alien registration card, known as a "green card." (At one time, the card was green, hence the name "green card.") The card permits registered aliens to work in the

After immigrants have fulfilled all of the legal requirements to become U.S. citizens, they are sworn in at public ceremonies such as this one.

United States. When the immigrant has lived in the United States for five years (or three years if the immigrant is married to a U.S. citizen), the immigrant can apply for citizenship. He or she is interviewed and must pass a test in U.S. government and history. A few months later, the person becomes a citizen at a public ceremony.

Issues of immigration remain controversial. Often opinions are so strongly felt that arguments are based on emotion rather than facts. Advocates of a generous immigration policy sometimes call their opponents racists and Fascists. Opponents of a generous policy sometimes call the supporters irresponsible or insensitive to the needs of the American people. An informed opinion about immigration policy needs to be based on facts and logic rather than emotion if the United States is to deal intelligently with this subject.

Chapter 3
THE IMMIGRANT POPULATION

Debate: Is the United States Admitting Too Many Immigrants?

In the 20th century, the nation has wrestled with the problem of deciding just how many people to allow in as immigrants. Public opinion polls in the 1990s show that between 60 to 80 percent of the American people want to reduce the number of immigrants to the United States. The idea that the United States is admitting too many immigrants is a view adopted in 1995 by the U.S. Commission on Immigration Reform, chaired by former Congresswoman Barbara Jordan. The commission recommended that the number of legal immigrants be reduced to 550,000 a year. As of 1997, Congress has not agreed to go along with that recommendation, however. Some organizations have even called for a halt in immigration—either on a temporary or permanent basis.

But the view that immigration numbers should be cut is far from unanimous because immigration continues to have its supporters. A *Wall Street Journal* editorial of July 3, 1984 stated: "If Washington still wants to 'do something' about immigration, we propose a five-word constitutional amendment: There shall be open borders."

DEBATED:

IS THE UNITED STATES ADMITTING TOO MANY IMMIGRANTS?

Yes. To argue that the nation is admitting too many immigrants is in no way to condemn the people from foreign countries who want to find a new life in a land of great opportunity and freedom. Yet, the United States, like other countries, has a right to control its own borders. In fact, it has an obligation to do so when the numbers of immigrants exceed the nation's capacity to absorb them properly, as is the case today. (Although the United States should reduce the number of both legal and illegal immigrants, this debate focuses on legal immigrants. Chapter 4 deals with illegal immigrants.)

The United States should reduce the number of immigrants for three reasons: (1) The number of immigrants is too high. (2) The United States cannot and should not solve its foreign policy problems through its immigration policy. (3) High immigration into the United States has a devastating impact on the environment not only for the United States but for the rest of the world, as well.

Numbers. The United States accepts more legal immigrants than the rest of the world combined. Most immigrants who come to the United States are relatives of U.S. citizens. In 1993, for example, 55 percent of immigrants were sponsored by a family member living in the United States. A reduction in the number of legal immigrants would in turn mean a reduction in the number of future immigrants because the need for family reunification would be much smaller than it is now.

The nation has been far too generous in its immigration policy in recent years. In the decades of the 1970s and 1980s, the United States admitted

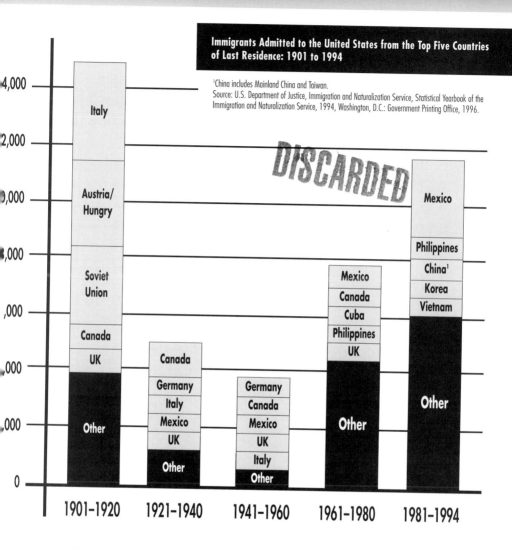

Immigrants Admitted to the United States from the Top Five Countries of Last Residence: 1901 to 1994

¹China includes Mainland China and Taiwan.
Source: U.S. Department of Justice, Immigration and Naturalization Service, Statistical Yearbook of the Immigration and Naturalization Service, 1994, Washington, D.C.: Government Printing Office, 1996.

10.7 million immigrants. As geographer Alvar W. Carlson notes: "This number is equivalent to the 1985 population of Ohio or that of countries such as Hungary or Portugal." By the mid-1990s, nearly 3,000 foreigners arrived to settle in the United States each day. In comparison, between 1901 and 1910, the United States admitted 8.8 million people. Economist George J. Borjas notes: "If present trends continue, as many as 10 million legal immigrants, and perhaps another 3 million illegals, will have entered the country in the 1990s." This would be the largest flow of immigrants in the United States for any decade in its history. The yearly population figures are striking, as Table 3.1 shows:

Table 3.1: Foreign-Born Population in the United States, 1970–1990

Year	Number (Millions)	% of Total U.S. Population
1970	9.6	4.7
1980	13.9	6.2
1990	19.8	7.9

Source: U.S. Bureau of the Census, Washington, D.C.

Even these figures for immigrants are misleading because they only include people who are given visas. Not part of these numbers are nonimmigrant workers, who are foreign nationals and who are legally entitled to work in the United States for specified periods of time. And the numbers do not include illegal immigrants.

Immigration is the driving force behind population growth in the United States. A close look at the demographic (population characteristics) figures shows an alarming fact: the birthrates of immigrants are higher than the birthrates of native-born Americans. One-third of the nation's net-population growth in the 1980s came from immigration. As Virginia D. Abernethy observes in her book *Population Politics*: "In California, where immigration from Mexico is a potent [powerful] factor, Hispanic fertility [the condition of being capable of producing offspring] rose from 3.16 in 1982, to 3.5 by 1988, and to over 3.9 in 1990." She also notes that native-born black women average 1.8 children, but foreign-born black women have 2.7 children. Other immigrant groups, such as South and Southeast Asians, Filipinos, and Russians, have large families, too. Writer Peter Brimelow calculates that if current immigration growth continues, U.S. population will reach 390 million in 2050, "of whom more than 130 million will be post-1970 immigrants and their descendants." Had there been no immigration after 1970, he adds, U.S. population would have stabilized in the range of 250 to 270 million.

A few words are in order about illegal immigration in this discussion of numbers because legal and illegal immigration are closely connected. Each year between 1.5 million and 2.5 million people enter the United States illegally. Most leave, but 300,000 remain.

California Governor Pete Wilson said in 1994 that there are one million illegal immigrants in Los Angeles alone, and that if the illegals there formed their own city, it would be the seventh largest city in the nation. He added that two-thirds of all babies born in Los Angeles public hospitals are born to illegal immigrants.

Legal immigration drives illegal immigration because often when illegals come to the United States, they have relatives and friends who encourage them to come and help them once they have entered the country. The help may be in the form of financial assistance, housing, and jobs. If legal immigration were reduced in size, then fewer illegals would be encouraged to come to the United States because their economic safety net would have been removed.

It is time to reduce the number of immigrants, as the Commission on Immigration Reform has urged. Reducing the number of legal immigrants is a good idea. Placing a moratorium (a suspension of action) on immigration for a few years until the United States can get its immigration policy and procedures in order is an even better idea.

Foreign policy. As the most powerful nation in the world, the United States must be involved in the problems of the world. It is a nation with military, economic, and humanitarian interests that are truly global. But there are limits to what the United States can do to solve the problems of the world because it already has too many of its own problems that it needs to solve. Sure, humanitarian goals are a legitimate purpose of U.S. foreign policy. It is moral and humane for the nation to allow into the United States refugees who have suffered from persecution and oppression. The United States should do what it can to help. The problem, however, is that if the United States were to admit every person who lived in a country that was unduly harsh toward its people, it would have to open its doors to more than a billion people.

To say that the United States should reduce the number of refugees admitted as immigrants is not to say that the United States should withdraw from providing diplomatic, military, and economic assistance to the victims of persecution, as the nation has done in such places as Somalia, Bosnia, Haiti, and Rwanda. There is a limit, however, to what the American people by themselves can do for the world.

U.S. willingness to accept so many immigrants from countries with nasty human rights problems may be harmful to the very nations that the United States should really try to help. By being so open to immigration from oppressed countries, the United States is removing from those countries the more energetic and disgruntled people, who, if not permitted entrance into the United States, would have to work within their own countries to bring down their oppressive political systems. Cuban Communist dictator Fidel

Castro understood this point very well and played the immigration game cleverly. In 1980, he permitted any Cubans who wished to leave Cuba to do so, and a great boatlift from the Cuban port of Mariel began in which 125,000 Cubans fled their homeland for the United States. Most Communist dictatorships have fallen, but Castro remained in power in part because he allowed the people with the greatest grievances to leave the country. He also emptied his prisons and let criminals and mentally ill Cubans join the boatlift, causing both criminal and financial problems for many American citizens.

There is a good deal of hypocrisy on the part of critics who say that U.S. immigration policy should set an example of world leadership. No other country has such idiotic immigration policies. Other countries correctly do not worry about world public opinion on the issue of immigration. In 1991, for example, Italy deported 20,000 Albanians. In recent years,

This overcrowded fishing boat was part of the boatlift from the port of Mariel to the United States that took place after Castro permitted those who wished to leave Cuba to do so.

Hong Kong and Singapore have deported Vietnamese boat people, who have fled their country because of political and economic factors. In 1996, African countries turned away Liberians who were fleeing from a breakdown of law and order in their African homeland.

Environment. In 1790, when the first U.S. census (an official count of population) was taken, about four million people made up the population of what was then the United States. Today, the population is more than 250 million. As mentioned earlier, the most dynamic element of that population growth is the increase in the number of immigrants since 1970. A continuing rise in the number of American people will have negative environmental consequences not only for the United States but also for the rest of the world.

The story of population growth and economic development shows the dangers ahead. When people move into an area, they need housing and work. Particularly in the United States, which is the most advanced industrial society in the world, people use a vast amount of consumer goods. And this use has consequences. New housing requires someone to provide the components, such as lumber and steel, for its construction. Items, such as stoves, freezers, air conditioning, computers, and television sets, that go into those homes also require basic resources. More housing means more land and water use. In a country that runs on wheels, moreover, more people means more automobiles. And more driving means more consumption of gas and oil and more production of air pollution. To find a place in the economy, new jobs must be created. New jobs mean more factories, increased development, and more use not only of the resources of the United States but of the rest of the world, as well.

There are already too many people on our planet in terms of the resources it possesses. The Earth is fragile and cannot sustain the ecosystem—the community of plants and animals and their environment that supply the raw materials for life—if it continues to overpopulate and if it does nothing to curb its seemingly endless use of resources for its consumer needs. Pollution, depletion (exhaustion) of resources, destruction of farmland, and loss of topsoil because of soil erosion—these are the environmental consequences of population increase. And the high and rising population of the United States is a chief cause of this environmental impoverishment.

Although the United States has less than 5 percent of the world's population, it consumes 30 percent of the world's resources. When immigrants come to the United States, they become the same kind of superconsumers as other Americans and in so doing contribute to environmental decay. Environment consultant Norman Myers makes some astonishing comparisons. He notes that the one billion people on the planet who live in developed countries may consume 100 times as much commercial energy as do most Bangladeshis, Ethiopians, and Bolivians. He adds: "In certain respects the additional 1.75 million Americans each year may well do as much damage to the biosphere [the area of the Earth and atmosphere where living things exist] as the 85 million additional Third Worlders."

The United States is causing increasing damage to the environment. It is exceeding its carrying capacity—the number of individuals that an area can support without sustaining damage. According to demographer (one who studies the characteristics of human population) Leon F. Bouvier and Lindsey Grant, Americans each year draw 25 percent more water from groundwater resources than gets replaced by nature. This development has led to irrigation problems and water shortages. The United States loses about 3 billion tons of topsoil each year and is tearing down its old-growth forests, destroying species of animals and plants in the process. Household and agricultural wastes are ruining wetlands (land areas that are saturated with moisture) and fisheries. And, according to Bouvier and Grant, the nation is having difficulty finding sufficient waste disposal sites and cannot handle the nuclear wastes that have been accumulating since the end of World War II.

The damage resulting from development takes a heavy toll on species of animals and plants. According to Charles A.S. Hall and his associates at the College of Environmental Science and Forestry at the State University of New York in Syracuse, there are 500,000 species in the United States, of which 6,000 are considered rare and endangered, or have been proposed for that listing. Hall and his associates explain: "Principal reasons are thought to be the growing human population in the United States and Americans' increasingly affluent [wealthy] lifestyle."

The nation is running out of resources, too. At present, the United States depends on fossil fuels (fuels such as coal, oil, or natural gases formed in the Earth from living matter from a previous geologic time) for its energy. But coal, which is available in abundance, is dirty and produces pollution. And the quantity of oil is limited. The nation relies on imported oil, much of it from the Middle East, which is a politically unstable region. If the United States is denied access to oil from abroad, as was the case after the Yom Kippur War in 1973, the United States would face severe economic hardship. It cannot turn to increasing its use of nuclear energy because it is too dangerous. In 1979, for example, a failure of the cooling system of a nuclear power plant at Three Mile Island in Pennsylvania, resulted in a partial meltdown of its uranium core. And in 1986, a nuclear accident occurred in Chernobyl in the Soviet Union, producing nuclear contamination throughout Eastern Europe and Scandinavia. Solar energy, which is produced from the sun, has not been perfected as a commercial energy source, and geothermal energy—the Earth's internal heat that is released naturally—does not make up a significant amount of the nation's energy resources. Attempts to turn to biomass—organic matter that can be converted to fuel—has its own problems. Biomass comes from farms or forests. The effort to convert corn into methanol, which is used in making gasoline, sounds like an environmentally friendly solution but it isn't. It requires more energy than it produces.

The environment is becoming subject to problems of global warming as a result of the release into the atmosphere of gases including carbon dioxide, methane, chlorofluorocarbons, and nitrous oxides. These gases trap heat, raising the temperature of the Earth, possibly producing what is known as a greenhouse effect. Because of the population growth in the United States, the nation will be using more energy, and in turn contributing to global warming. Some scientists observe that human-made pollutants, such as chlorofluorocarbons, are destroying the ozone layer. Ozone is a gas. In the stratosphere (the upper portion of the atmosphere), it forms a layer that helps to prevent most ultraviolet and other radiation harmful to Earth from penetrating to the surface of the Earth. The thinning of the ozone layer increases the chance of people getting cancer.

As the population increases, so does the number of automobiles on the road, which means greater gas and oil consumption, and more air pollution.

Humans have also added to the pollution problem with acid rain, which is produced when sulfur dioxide and nitrogen oxides combine with moisture. Acid rain can pollute drinking water, damage vegetation, and kill fish. It has been a problem in the United States, Canada, and Europe.

Development in the United States not only harms the ecosystem in the United States but does great damage to the environment in other countries, as well. For example, deforestation—the clearing of forests—has caused damage to the environment in tropical countries. The depletion of oil and natural resources in other countries proceeds because of the demands for goods coming from the United States. A reduction in immigration to the United States would be an environmentally good policy not only for the United States but also for the rest of the world.

The American people wisely favor a reduction in legal immigration, as poll after poll shows. They well understand that the number of immigrants is too high. Immigrants have made great contributions to America, but the nation has reached its limits as to how many people it can take in. The United States should not abandon its concern for people in other nations. But it can show its concern through means other than immigration, such as through economic, humanitarian, and diplomatic assistance. Reducing the number of immigrants, moreover, will have beneficial environmental consequences.

No.
Immigrant-bashing is much in fashion these days, as immigrants are blamed for so many of the problems of crime, unemployment, and pollution that are present in the United States. If we listen to the critics of immigration, we would expect that all of our great problems will either be solved or greatly reduced when the nation turns its back on the very people who want to make the United States even greater than it has become. The United States is not admitting too many immigrants. In fact, we can easily admit more. The nation, too, has a national interest in welcoming newcomers, and a cutback in immigration will suggest to the world that the United States will return to a policy of isolationism. Finally, the fears that immigrants are contributing to environmental horrors lack a basis in fact.

Numbers. To begin with, the United States does not have a problem of admitting too many immigrants. Although the number of foreign-born persons in the United States is at an all-time high, the percentage of the population that is foreign-born is only 8 percent, according to the U.S. census in 1990. In order to provide historical perspective, let's take a look at Table 3.2, which provides some longer-range figures than those of merely the period between 1970 and 1990.

Table 3.2: Foreign-Born Population in the United States, 1920–1990

Year	Number (Millions)	% of Total U.S. Population
1920	14.0	13.2
1930	14.2	11.6
1940	11.6	8.8
1950	10.4	6.9
1960	9.7	5.4
1970	9.6	4.7
1980	13.9	6.2
1990	19.8	7.9

Source: U.S. Bureau of the Census, Washington, D.C.

As the table shows, in 1920, the foreign-born population was 13.2 percent of the U.S. population compared to the 7.9 percent foreign-born population in 1990. If we go back earlier than 1920, the figures are even more striking. In the period between 1870 and 1920, nearly 15 percent of the U.S. population was foreign-born. So the only important fact that we should keep in mind is that immigrants make up a smaller proportion of the American people than they did a century ago.

It is true that the United States has the highest population of any major industrialized country, but it can in no way be regarded as overpopulated or likely to become so in the near future. If overpopulation is measured in terms of population per square mile, the United States may be described as underpopulated. For example, here are some figures of the population per square kilometer of surface area in some countries for 1990: Japan, 327; Belgium, 323; Italy, 189; Greece, 76; and Ireland 50. The comparable figure for the United States is 27.

Foreign policy. The United States is the strongest and most influential power in the world. This was not always the case. In the 20 years following World War I, it pursued a policy of isolationism. But the rise of Germany, Italy, and Japan and the coming of World War II showed that the United States had to pursue a policy of engagement in world affairs. And so it did through its participation in that war. With a world shattered by the horrors of that great war, the only country that could challenge the Soviet Union, the strongest power in Europe that was threatening other countries, was the United States. And the United States became the leader of the alliance that triumphed over communism with the breakup of the Soviet Union in 1991. U.S. leadership required not only military strength but moral strength, as well, because the conflict between the superpowers had as much to do with moral power as it did with military power. The conflict between the superpowers was a war over ideas and values.

The United States showed from its actions that it had a genuine concern for the well-being of people who were victims of Communist dictatorships. When the Soviet Union intervened in Hungary in 1956 to put down an independence movement, the United States opened its borders to accept Hungarian refugees. Cubans angry about the dictatorship under Castro were also given refuge in the United States. In hindsight, many Americans regretted the unwillingness of the United States to admit the victims of Adolf Hitler's brutal Nazi regime in the 1930s by opening its borders to Jews and others who, as a result of their remaining in Germany, went to their deaths in extermination camps.

Although the cold war is over, the United States still faces challenges from other powers, as its war with Iraq in 1991 demonstrates. Efforts to shut the door to victims of oppression and to those who wish to work and find a place in an economy of great opportunity only lead to criticism of the United States and undermine U.S. leadership in the world. The fact that so many people trying unsuccessfully to enter the country are nonwhite, particularly Asian and Hispanic people, produces accusations of racism against the United States—a charge that can only harm U.S. foreign policy.

Sure, the United States has many means other than adopting a liberal immigration policy to engage with other countries. It properly uses economic, military, and diplomatic tools to achieve its goals. But those are not enough to win the hearts and minds of people of other nations. Particularly since family reunification is so central to U.S. immigration policy, it would be heartless to deny Americans the opportunity to have their family loved ones join them in this country. The result of reducing the number of legal immigrants would only strengthen anti-American sentiment abroad and harm the United States in its relations with other countries.

Environment. Environmentalist fears that the world is in danger of extinction because it has too many people in terms of existing resources is a view that is at least two centuries old. The early originator of this view was Thomas Malthus, an English economist who in 1798 wrote *An Essay on the Principle of Population.* In that work, Malthus argued that poverty and distress are inevitable because population increases faster than the means to keep people alive. The modern followers of Malthus—or neo-Malthusians as they are sometimes called—make similar charges.

But the evidence since Malthus wrote shows that he was wrong. World population has increased from 1 billion people in the early 19th century to over 5 billion at the end of the 20th century. Yet many people in the world live long and healthy lives. The standard of living for the masses of people of the industrialized and industrializing countries is rising, not falling. China and India are successively the two most populous countries in the world. Yet their economies are booming. Life expectancy, standard of living, and quality of health of the people of these countries have improved as these nations have industrialized since the end of World War II. To be sure, pockets of poverty remain in these countries, but so, too, do they remain even in advanced industrial societies. What Malthus and the neo-Malthusians failed to take into account is the importance of human intelligence in applying science and technology to increasing and improving the material goods of the world.

True, there are famines in the world. When they are produced by natural forces, such as earthquakes, floods, and droughts, other nations are usually capable of stepping in to provide humanitarian assistance. But often the famines are caused by political factors, such as civil war or efforts by a dictator to take away the property of peasants who own their land. There is no reason why the benefits from science and technology will not continue to be applied to raise the standard of living of impoverished peoples throughout the world, so long as political conditions encourage investment and individual initiative.

Neo-Malthusians claim that the United States has a farmland crisis as a result of the overuse of land, soil erosion, and water shortages. And yet economic history seems to tell us not to be alarmed. At the beginning of the 20th century, about half of the population of the United States was engaged in agriculture and produced enough food for its people. Today, with less land available, 2 percent of the nation's population produces enough food to feed not only Americans but many people throughout the rest of the world, as well.

It is true, as neo-Malthusians claim, that modern technology is using resources at a faster rate than ever before. But the idea that we cannot find solutions to current environmental problems is without a basis in fact. We can extend the use of existing resources through recycling. In the great consumer societies, such as the United States and Germany, recycling has become a legal requirement in many instances. For example, people who dispose of their garbage must by law separate their "garbage" so that such items as newspapers, bottles, and aluminum containers can be reprocessed.

We can solve the other problems that critics of population growth in general and immigration growth in particular are complaining about. Environmental laws are already in place that have improved the quality of air and water in many parts of America. Lead is an excellent example of the importance of environmental laws. Lead can have a harmful effect on the learning ability of children. The United States adopted laws that brought down yearly emissions (discharges) of lead from more than 200,000 tons in 1970 to about 10,000 tons in 1989. Environmental laws reduced sulfur dioxide emissions by 26 percent, and carbon monoxide by 40 percent in the same time frame.

Fears that the nation is running out of resources, such as energy, are unfounded, too. At present, oil companies are prevented from mining oil because of legal restrictions created by the efforts of environmentalists. This has happened, for example, in parts of Alaska, which is rich in oil. Developments in geothermal energy and solar energy show promise for future energy use. In addition, the United States and many other countries can rely on nuclear energy. So long as the processing of nuclear energy remains safe, the United States has a virtually unlimited source of energy. Nuclear energy is safe and does not produce air pollution. The problem at Three Mile Island did not result in any deaths. And the disaster at Chernobyl was caused by inattention to basic safety procedures.

Talk about the disasters that loom ahead is exaggerated. We hear about the ozone layer thinning, but we see no evidence that this development directly produces an increasing number of diseases. Agricultural production continues to rise in spite of claims about global warming. Acid rain has only produced limited damage. Economist Julian L. Simon notes: "It may even be that a greenhouse effect would benefit us on balance by warming some areas we'd like warmer, and by increasing the carbon dioxide to agriculture."

The fact is that we do not know a good deal about changing climate conditions. Scientists disagree about it. In the 1960s and 1970s, scientists were worried about global cooling, not global warming. Although carbon dioxide in the atmosphere has increased in recent decades, scientists disagree about the effect of this increase on global temperature. They disagree, too, about the areas of the world it would affect and whether it would be more serious than an unexpected change in the weather.

Similar remarks need to be made about the ozone layer. It is true that the ozone layer is thinning. But some scientists say that this situation results from natural developments, such as volcanic ash and sunspots. Before we change public policy and destroy jobs or limit immigration, we need to be sure of the facts. We should not panic and in the process harm human beings.

Reports about the loss of species are exaggerated. Biologists are not in agreement about the number of species that will become extinct, with pessimists claiming numbers of extinct species in the hundreds each year and projections reaching as high as 40,000 by the year 2000. But we really do not know the number.

It is clear that species have disappeared before, but often the loss of the species has not been disastrous and may even be beneficial. In this respect, Julian L. Simon asks: "What kinds of species may have been extinguished when the [U.S.] settlers clear-cut the Middle West of the United States? Could we be much the poorer now for their loss?" He concludes: "Obviously we do not know the answers. But it seems hard to even imagine that we would be enormously better off with the persistence of any such imagined species. This casts some doubt on the economic value that might be lost elsewhere."

We need not fear an increase in legal immigration because of environmental concerns, then. We have plenty of land and great technology to get ever higher yields of farm products. We have sufficient resources to exploit, and we can do so safely so long as the nation complies with environmental-protection laws. Immigrants are no threat to the environment.

There is no need to reduce the number of legal immigrants that the United States admits each year. The facts show that a smaller proportion of U.S. citizens are foreign-born today than was the case at the beginning of the 20th century. The standard of living has risen in this century and is continuing to rise as our population increases. It is well within the foreign policy interest of the United States to welcome immigrants as we have in past years. And we need not fear that maintaining the number of legal immigrants in the United States will cause any environmental damage.

Chapter 4
ILLEGAL IMMIGRATION

Debate: Should the United States Establish
A National Employment Verification System?

On June 6, 1993, a freighter, the *Golden Venture*, ran aground off the shore of Rockaway Beach, New York. On board the ship were 282 Chinese nationals who were being smuggled out of China by an organized crime smuggling group. In an effort to avoid arrest, some of the passengers jumped into the water and tried to swim ashore. Six drowned. Five escaped, uncaught by Immigration and Naturalization Service (INS) agents and inspectors. But the remaining 271 passengers were taken into custody by INS officials. Some of the passengers had paid as much as $30,000 to people who provided the means for them to make the trip. U.S. immigration officials had most of the survivors deported. The story of the *Golden Venture* was not a unique event in attempted illegal entry into the United States. Every year, an estimated 1.25 million people try to enter the United States illegally—a rate of more than two per minute.

It is easy for legal foreign visitors to come into the United States. As a free and open society, the United States offers many opportunities for people to do so. Foreign students who study, tourists who visit vacation retreats, and businesspeople who have commercial interests in the United States arrive daily. Government officials have a difficult job even inspecting people coming into the United States because they not only have to inspect the papers of foreign visitors, but they have to do the same for returning U.S. citizens, as well. The U.S. Commission on Immigration Reform reports that in 1993, approximately 409 million people were inspected at U.S. land ports of entry, 55 million at airports, and 9 million at seaports.

Many foreign citizens who become illegal aliens actually enter the United States legally by air. They have permission to visit the United States for a few months. Once here, however, they stay on indefinitely, becoming illegal immigrants. In addition, some foreign individuals who arrive at a large U.S. airport claim that they are persecuted at home, and apply for political asylum. Because there is a backlog of cases involving asylum, these asylees are set free in the United States on parole because the INS, the government unit most responsible for enforcing immigration laws, does not have facilities to house them. In 1994, there was a backlog of 400,000 asylum cases waiting to be heard. Under current rules, applicants are given work authorization and can legally remain in the United States for extended periods. They enter the United States pending a hearing to evaluate their claim. Many then do not return for the hearing. Only 10 to 15

Immigration officers stand near the freighter *Golden Venture* after the ship, which was trying to smuggle Asian illegal immigrants, ran aground.

percent of those who attend their hearings are granted asylum. In January 1994, however, the Clinton administration ended the policy of granting a work authorization card immediately upon applying for asylum. The policy now requires applicants to wait for six months to receive the card. The Clinton administration also increased the number of asylum officers and immigration judges. The result was that the number of people who came forward on their own to request asylum fell by more than half in a single year. The number of people who requested asylum after the immigration service caught them and moved to deport them also dropped.

An immigration law of 1996 tightened requirements for asylum seekers. It provides for a one-year time limit after entry for those who apply for political asylum, with some exceptions. In addition, if a person seeking asylum is found to have no believable fear of persecution after an initial meeting with an INS officer, the person is subject to removal after a hearing before an immigration judge. The hearing must take place within seven days and cannot be appealed.

Many who are illegal immigrants do not enter the United States legally, however. The United States has borders extending 6,000 miles (9,650 km), a distance so great that law-enforcement officials have difficulty securing its territory against those people who want to enter illegally. The border between Texas and Mexico alone is 868 miles (1,400 km) long and easy to penetrate. The Border Patrol, the federal unit that tries to prevent illegals from entering the country, reports that it captured 1.25 million people trying to enter the United States illegally in 1993. But it estimates that two out of three who tried to come in illegally that year succeeded in doing so.

Some aliens try to make it by ship, as the case of the *Golden Venture* shows. And many come in by foot across the Mexican-U.S. border. Not all illegals who cross the Mexican border are Mexican nationals, however. Some come from Albania, China, Yugoslavia, Poland, Turkey, Ghana, Pakistan, and India. Others come from Central America. Most who come in illegally from Mexico do not do so on their own. For a payment of $200 or more per person, they use the services of a "coyote," who is a professional smuggler of immigrants into the United States familiar with the best routes to cross undetected. The dangers of the trip are great. Some would-be illegals are robbed, raped, or murdered. Some drown in unseaworthy boats. Others are abandoned when there is danger of arrest. Even when they make it into the United States, they are always in fear that INS officials will find and deport them.

But many who make the journey succeed in getting through. The INS estimates that in 1992 there were 3.4 million "permanent" illegal aliens in the United States. Of this amount, about half entered legally by air and overstayed their visas. The other half came in by land or sea without inspection. Some private estimates put the figure of permanent illegal aliens as high as 5.4 million.

Some illegals come for a short period of time, but some seek to settle here. For $25 to $50, they obtain phony identification credentials, such as a work permit, Social Security card, or a driver's license, from criminals who furnish those documents. They find housing, sometimes with friends or relatives, and, at other times, in trailer camps that cater to immigrants. And they look for and find jobs, too—a process that is not all that difficult, in part because the laws against hiring illegal immigrants have weaknesses. The IRCA of 1986, for example, makes it a crime, punishable by fines and jail terms, for an employer to knowingly hire an illegal worker. The law requires the employer to make a good-faith effort to inspect the documents from job applicants. The employer may accept as proof of identity and work eligibility two of 29 documents, including a birth certificate. But if the documents are fake, the employer is not legally liable for punishment unless he or she knows that they are fake. Since the 1986 law, the number of documents acceptable for identity and work eligibility has been slightly reduced.

The federal government has taken steps to deal with illegals. It increased agents in the Border Patrol. It strengthened fortifications, too. For example, it built a 14-mile (23-km) long and 10-foot (3-m) high steel barricade south of San Diego, California, a major transit area for illegals coming from Mexico. It adapted new tactics aimed at preventing illegals from crossing the border rather than capturing them once they are across the border.

One of the major goals of those who wish to put an end to illegal immigration is to find a truly effective way to stop illegals from getting jobs. In this regard, the INS has already begun pilot (testing) programs to test the status of job seekers in an effort to locate illegal workers. A pilot program in California involved as many as 234 companies and tourist attractions, including Brinks, Inc.; Disneyland; and Knott's Berry Farms. The employers checked the job applications of 11,400 people who identified themselves as noncitizens and learned that 3,000, approximately 25 percent, did not have valid work papers. And in May 1996, the Clinton administration expanded the program to include the nation's four largest meatpacking companies by using a computerized data system at 41 plants in 12 states to determine if job applicants are legal workers. This industry has attracted a large number of illegal workers. These programs are voluntary, however.

Here illegals help one another climb over a wall along the Mexico-U.S. border. The Border Patrol estimates that in 1993, two out of three illegals who tried to enter the United States succeeded.

The 1996 immigration law provides for improved verification procedures. Pilot programs will be established in five states that are known to have illegal immigrant problems. In these programs, employers can voluntarily check the legal status of prospective workers through a Justice Department program.

Rather than rely on voluntary measures, some public officials have recommended doing something to prevent illegal immigrants from obtaining phony papers that allow them to work. The U.S. Commission on Immigration Reform, among others, has called for a central data bank that employers would use to verify that an applicant for a job has documents that are in fact legal, rather than merely look legal.

Those calling for the establishment of some kind of new verification system have suggested three ways of going about it: (1) Designate the Social Security card as the sole document for proof of both an employee's identity and work eligibility. (2) Enable employers to verify the employment eligibility status through an automated Alien Status Verification Index data bank that can be accessed by telephone. (3) Require the Social Security Administration to validate (prove the truth) in advance a job applicant's Social Security number before a state issues a driver's license or other state identification cards. These procedures are designed to establish a national employment verification system.

DEBATED:

SHOULD THE UNITED STATES ESTABLISH A NATIONAL EMPLOYMENT VERIFICATION SYSTEM?

Yes. Illegal immigration is out of control as foreigners who are inclined to live in the United States in violation of the law find that they can get around the laws without fear of punishment. The availability of false identification papers makes their task rather easy. An employer who wants to comply with the law is not a detective and lacks access to methods of verifying that the documents a job applicant presents are authentic. That is why the Commission on Immigration Reform has called for a central data bank by which employers could verify whether foreign workers are properly documented. Others have called for similar measures. Pilot projects are underway. The purpose of the pilot programs is to determine which system would be best to prevent fraud without interfering with people's privacy and without encouraging discrimination. A national employment verification system would be an excellent measure that would reduce the number of illegal immigrants and, at the same time, protect individual liberties.

Necessary. Jobs are the magnets that attract illegal immigration. A national employment verification system is necessary because the current system of verifying the identity and status of job applicants is not working. If a secure identification system could be drawn up, then illegal immigrants will be truly undocumented workers and will be unable to find work in the United States—at least not legally. Many foreigners thinking about coming to the United States to find work would no doubt be discouraged from going through the expense and the danger of even entering the United States because they would face a dim employment future.

In enacting the IRCA in 1986, Congress hoped to close off employment opportunities by illegals. But the method of checking a job seeker's documents has proved to be fatally flawed. According to the IRCA, 29 different kinds of documents could be accepted as proof to verify an applicant's identity and authorization to work. The documents include U.S. passports, Alien Registration Receipt Cards, birth certificates, voter registration cards, and Social Security cards that do not have a nonwork legend. Some of these documents, such as a U.S. passport, can be accepted to establish both employment eligibility and identity. Others, such as the Social Security card, have to be accompanied by another document, such as a state driver's license. Typical documents are a driver's license for identity and a Social Security card for employment.

A problem with this kind of identification is that employers have no easy way to verify that they are authentic. Existing documents that are acceptable can be easily falsified. For example, there is no nationally standardized method to issue birth certificates or copies of birth certificates. In many states, birth certificates may be issued by local offices, county clerks, local officials, and even librarians. The format of the birth certificate varies from one state to another. And the requirements for issuing a certified copy of a birth certificate also differ from state to state. A national system of employment verification is necessary to reduce opportunities for engaging in fraud to obtain work.

Practical. A verifiable system of identification is practical. The American people already rely on very practical and easy means of identification in going about their daily business. A person seeking to withdraw money from a bank finds it easy to use an automatic machine requiring a bank card and a personal identification number to do so. Often, the process is even faster than standing in line waiting for a bank teller to deal with an account. A customer in a department store or a supermarket hands a credit card to a salesperson who then places the card in an electronic device that establishes in seconds that the card is authentic.

A central data bank for determining employment eligibility could be just as efficient and accurate as a bank card or credit card. If a secure Social Security card became the chief source of identification, then an employer would use the telephone or an automatic verification electronic system to the Social Security office or other government unit to find out whether the card was authentic. If the information coming back indicated that the Social Security number was invalid, then the applicant for the job would be told to report to the appropriate office to clear up the matter.

Of course, devising a new system will not be cheap. The Department of Labor estimates that the cost of a verification system using telephone calls to a government data bank would average $33 million a year for the first five years and about $200 million per year thereafter. Doubling the number of INS investigators would add $25 to $30 million. But the costs are really not high. Evaluating these figures, Dan Stein, executive director of the Federation for Immigration Reform, notes: "Thus, a new system to verify work eligibility clearly will not exceed in cost the amount directly saved as a result of reduced public assistance alone [to illegal immigrants], not even considering the value of the other benefits of reducing illegal immigration."

Privacy. The new system would allow for privacy. At present, an employer asks a potential employee to complete an I-9 form, which is the Employment Eligibility Verification Form, and to produce identification. The new system can in effect obtain similar information through the data bank. It will contain only enough information to verify that the Social Security number is valid and has been issued to a person legally permitted to work in the United States. Some critics argue that the new employer verification card will become a national identity card that individuals will be required to carry and produce on demand by law-enforcement officials. But an employment verification card is not a national identity card any more than a driver's license is a national identity card.

Current law protects individuals against violations of privacy. The Privacy Act of 1974 specifies the conditions under which government records may be disclosed, the kinds of information that a government agency may place in records, and the ability of an individual to gain access to his or her records. Under Section 3 of this act, a government agency cannot disclose any record that is contained in a system of any records to any person or group without the written consent of the individual to whom the record pertains. It also requires that an agency collect only the information necessary by law to fulfill the purposes of that agency in carrying out the law. The IRCA also has safeguards limiting the information that can be used.

It is true that modern life requires people to provide a good deal of information about themselves, but society is able to deal with that. Access to credit reports and medical records is limited by law. A police officer may require the driver of a vehicle to produce a driver's license. But the officer has no right to ask a pedestrian to produce a driver's license. Similarly, a work identification card can be limited in use to do exactly what is intended: to prove that the holder is eligible to work.

A national system of employer verification relying on a central data bank would prevent discrimination and replace the current system, which encourages discrimination. With the present system, if job seekers are Hispanic or Asian, some employers do not consider hiring them. They fear that the applicants' documents will be phony because of the high numbers of immigrants who are Hispanic or Asian. In 1990, the General Accounting Office (GAO), an investigatory arm of Congress, found that "a widespread pattern of discrimination has resulted against eligible workers." In its random survey of more than 4.6 million employers in 1990, it estimated that 891,000 or 19 percent of the surveyed population, admitted to practicing discrimination because of IRCA: 461,000 reported national origin discrimination; and 430,000 employers reported citizenship discrimination. And 76 percent of the employers who in the survey said that they began a practice of hiring only U.S.-born persons reported that they did not have any Hispanic or Asian employees. The GAO concluded that "many employers discriminated because the law's verification system does not provide a simple or reliable method to verify job applicants' eligibility to work."

The Commission on Immigration Reform correctly notes that the existence of a system of identification from a central database would prevent discrimination. An employer would not even have to ask an applicant if he or she is an immigrant. Producing the card would be required of all applicants, just as the Social Security card is required today. Minorities—particularly Hispanics and Asians, who are citizens or aliens with work permits—would now be more likely to be employed rather than experience the unfairness of discrimination.

It is clear that the current system of worker identification makes the hope of those who wrote the IRCA a failure. The law has been undermined by the existence of false documents that permit illegal immigrants an opportunity to find work. If the nation is ever going to get a handle on the illegal immigration problem, it must adopt a national system of employment verification.

No. The United States needs to control its borders. It should take reasonable steps to deal with the flow of illegal immigrants. But the proposal to establish a national employment verification system is unreasonable. It is unnecessary, impractical, and invades privacy.

Unnecessary. That the United States has a problem of illegal immigration cannot be denied. But a national employment verification system is unnecessary because there are other and more effective ways to deal with the problem. More vigorous law enforcement is one way. More inspectors need to be hired to investigate violations of existing laws. Already, the Border Patrol has hired more agents and has increased the number of arrests of illegals crossing the Mexican-U.S. border. Constructing more fences along the Mexican-U.S. border would help reduce the flow of illegal immigrants, also.

A major reason why illegal immigrants come to the United States is economics. Illegal immigrants search for jobs in the United States because they lack work opportunity in their own countries. If they could find jobs in their own countries, then they would not be likely to leave. The United States should encourage U.S. investment to build the economies of other nations. As a giant economic power, it can use its vast wealth to help not only private U.S. investors in search of profits but poor people who are willing to work hard. The result of such investment would be to reduce the need to emigrate.

Impractical. A national system of employment verification is highly impractical to establish. It is costly, too. The Social Security card is a case in point. According to a report in 1992 by the Subcommittee on Immigration and Refugee Affairs of the House Committee on the Judiciary, over 300 million Social Security numbers have been issued on 16 different valid versions of the Social Security card since the card was introduced in 1936. Estimates are that there are 250 million active Social Security numbers today. But over 60 percent of these cards were issued without proof of the individual's identity or citizenship.

The documents used to obtain a Social Security card, then, are not secure. There is no photograph on the card, and it is easily forged. In addition, the Social Security Administration makes errors in bookkeeping and data entry. To make a national employment verification system based on the Social Security card would require a huge bureaucratic effort, which would no doubt turn out to produce inaccuracies in many cases.

Documents other than Social Security cards lack a national standard. There is no national standard for birth and baptismal certificates, driver's licenses, school records, and medical records. The Commissioner of Social Security said in 1991 that a more secure Social Security card would cost between $1.5 and $2.5 billion. Testifying before a House subcommittee in 1994, Lawrence H. Thompson, Deputy Commissioner, Social Security Administration, said: "Reissuing [Social Security] cards to the entire population could run easily from $3 billion to as much as $6 billion in one-time costs, most of that associated not with the new cards, but with the process of verifying identity all over again."

No doubt a new verification system would require cooperation between many agencies of government, such as the Social Security Administration, the INS, and the Department of Labor. But government agencies dealing with large numbers of people make mistakes. For example, the *New York Times* reported: "A recent search of 3.5 million INS records resulted in misidentification of 65,000 persons who actually were lawfully present in the U.S." Many people who are misidentified will no doubt suffer.

Privacy. The problem of a national employment verification system is that it is a first step to creating a national identity card, which is associated more with the needs of a dictatorship to pry into the affairs of ordinary citizens rather than the needs of a democracy to respect the rights and privacy of its people. The history of the Social Security number warns us what to expect.

When Social Security was started, Congress avoided a national identity card by restricting the use of the Social Security number. But starting in the 1940s, the Social Security number became in effect a national identification number. President Franklin D. Roosevelt issued Executive Order 9397 in 1943, which encouraged federal agencies to use the Social Security number when establishing a "new system of government account numbers pertaining to individual persons." In 1961, the Civil Service Commission used the Social Security number to identify all federal employees, and in 1966, the Internal Revenue Service (IRS), the federal agency responsible for collecting federal taxes, required it for all individual tax returns. Today, Social Security numbers are being used by state agencies to locate deadbeat fathers who have stopped paying child support. In effect, the Social Security card is a national identification card.

With knowledge of someone's Social Security number, one can find out much about a person's financial holdings, credit records, and medical history. It is not surprising that when President Bill Clinton reveals his income tax information to the public, he deletes his Social Security number. No doubt the President understands the misuse that people can make of that number.

If the new employment verification card, backed up by a central data bank, is put into effect, it will be even more of an invasion of privacy than the Social Security card. It will be used to concentrate too much information about each person who has one. Not only will it contain information necessary for employment, but it is likely to have other information on confidential matters, such as personal health and finances. Law-enforcement agencies, such as the Federal Bureau of Investigation and state and local police, as well as the IRS and the Central Intelligence Agency, would all gain as a result of the new system. All of these government organizations have on occasions engaged in activities that have violated the privacy rights of citizens and noncitizens. No doubt, they will have an even easier time to invade the privacy of citizens through use of such a card.

If an employment verification card comes into effect, individuals will learn too late that private information may be sent to users outside of government for purposes that have nothing to do with obtaining a job. The idea of a government having that kind of information about its citizens is in conflict with the values of freedom that are enshrined in the Constitution.

It is reasonable to expect that the new card will be used to check the identity of people who look "foreign," particularly Asians and Hispanics. Incidents of racial discrimination will likely increase because of this development. One can expect that if a police official finds a suspicious person, the official will ask that person to produce the national employment verification card. If the person does not have it, the police official might detain or arrest the individual, who is now a suspect. Loss of privacy, then, will be produced by a national employment verification card.

The United States has a real problem of illegal immigration. But requiring a national employment verification policy creates problems of necessity, practicality, and privacy that make the proposed system a bad idea.

The Social Security card is fairly simple to fraudulently produce.

Chapter 5
IMMIGRATION AND THE ECONOMY

Debate: Is Immigration Bad for the Economy?

Although the United States has been guided at times by humanitarian concerns in its immigration policy, the principal driving force behind immigration has been the belief that immigration is good for the nation's economy. A growing labor force helped the United States become a giant both in agriculture and in industry. Immigrants harvested the crops, worked in the mines and factories, built the railroads, and created new businesses.

But Americans have not been in agreement about the value of immigrants in strengthening the nation's economy. Particularly during difficult periods of great economic distress, such as depressions and recessions, American citizens who have difficulty finding jobs or who see their wages kept low because of competition from a seemingly unlimited supply of workers from other countries favor stopping the flow of immigrants to the United States. In the 19th century, many Americans (some of whom were immigrants themselves or children of immigrants) turned against Chinese immigrants in part because of a feeling that the Chinese were a threat to their jobs and livelihood. In the late 20th century, some Americans turn against Mexican and other immigrants from Latin America and the Caribbean as well as from Asia for similar reasons.

DEBATED:

IS IMMIGRATION BAD FOR THE ECONOMY?

Yes. The issue of whether immigration is bad for the economy is best judged by the impact of immigration on economic growth, jobs, and welfare. It is clear from such an analysis that immigration is harmful in each respect.

Economic growth. Economic growth may mean an increase in the size of a nation's output (goods produced) or in the per capita income of the people in a nation. If immigration is such an engine for economic growth, we would expect to see nations that are highly receptive to immigrants to be experiencing high growth, and nations that are not receptive to immigrants as experiencing low or no growth. But such is not the case. Japan with a population of 125 million (about half that of the United States) has almost no immigration, but it has become the second-largest economy in the world. As writer Peter Brimelow notes: "GDP (gross domestic product) [the value of all goods and services produced within a country's boundaries in a specific period of time]...is up nearly ten times since 1955 [in Japan], and is now about perhaps half that of the United States, which has barely tripled in the same period...."

It is true that the nation experienced economic growth throughout its history, but immigration was not the cause of economic expansion. The United States would have done equally as well without immigration. It was a manufacturing country by 1850—before the great waves of immigration. Moreover, except for the period of the Great Depression of the 1930s, the United States had greater prosperity between 1914 and 1965 than it has ever had. This was a period in which immigration was severely restricted.

Even if one can make a strong case for immigration as a force for economic growth in the past, one cannot make that case today. It is true that immigrants helped build American economic strength. But the conditions that produced that strength are no longer with us. Until the 20th century, the United States needed mostly energetic and unskilled labor, much of which was supplied by immigrants. Agriculture required the largest percentage of the workforce. And the factories relied on manpower to fulfill the needs of assembly lines. Essentially, the strength of the economy was built on the muscle power of the labor force.

Today, however, conditions are different. Science and technology contributed to the increasing replacement of workers with machinery and robots in both agriculture and industry. Agriculture now accounts for about 2 percent of the U.S. workforce. Today, the economic strength of the nation relies on fewer workers to manufacture products than were required earlier. The kinds of people the United States now needs in its economy are those who are skilled and educated. Since 1965, however, immigration law has encouraged "family reunification" rather than skill and education. According to economist George J. Borjas: "More recent immigrant waves have relatively less schooling, lower earnings, lower labor force participation rates, and higher poverty rates than earlier waves had at similar stages of their assimilation into the country. Therefore, the nature of the skill sorting generated by the immigration market has deteriorated substantially in recent years."

It is sometimes said that many immigrants are entrepreneurs (people willing to take risks in business ventures) and create jobs because of their business talent. But in 1990, only 6.8 percent of immigrant workers were self-employed, compared to 7 percent of native workers, according to Census Bureau statistics. It is true that some ethnic groups have high representation among entrepreneurs, but others do not. Borjas notes in this regard: "Only 6 percent of Vietnamese immigrants, 5 percent of Mexican immigrants, and 3 percent of Filipino immigrants were self-employed."

The sad commentary is that the focus of admitting immigrants into the United States has moved away from economic considerations, which is not surprising given the shift in the organizational structure of government in dealing with immigration. When immigration policy became the sole responsibility of the federal government with the enactment of the Immigration Act of 1891 (it had been the responsibility of both the federal and state governments before then), the Bureau of Immigration was established in the Department of the Treasury. The INS was made part of the Department of Labor in 1914 when the department was created and remained in that department until 1940 when it was transferred to the Department of Justice. The Labor Department viewed immigration from the point of working people's interest in contrast to the Justice Department, which views it from its perspective of law enforcement.

Jobs. Business groups are key supporters of immigration. It is not surprising, therefore, that immigration serves business interests at the expense of worker interests. Immigrants may cause the greatest economic damage to unskilled workers. In 1986, the President's Council on Economic Advisors summarized these effects: "Although immigrant workers increase output, their addition to the supply of labor...[causes] wage rates in the immediately affected market [to be] bid down.... Thus, native-born workers who compete with immigrants for jobs may experience reduced earnings or reduced employment."

In an article in the political magazine *Dissent* published in 1993, economics writer Richard Rothstein told the story of residential drywallers (the workers who erect plasterboard for interior home walls) in the late 1970s, who were members of the carpenters' union in southern California. They earned on average about $1,100 a week and received health insurance, pension, and vacation benefits. By 1982, contractors began to hire nonunion Mexican immigrants and stopped hiring union drywallers. The contractors eliminated the health insurance, pension, and vacation benefits and reduced the wages that they had been paying. Although the workers gained back some benefits and a wage increase as a result of bringing legal action, they now receive only about half of what nonimmigrant workers earned a decade earlier.

The case of the drywallers is not unique to our times. Immigration has always taken a heavy toll on unskilled African-American workers. African-American leaders have historically been concerned about the impact of immigration on black people. The great opponent of slavery Frederick Douglass wrote in 1871 before the great migration from Eastern and Southern Europe: "The former slaveowners of the South want cheap labor; they want it from Germany and from Ireland; they want it from China and Japan; they want it from anywhere in the world but from Africa. They want to be independent of their former slaves, and bring their noses to the grindstone."

And in his famous speech at the Atlanta Exposition of 1895, Booker T. Washington, the influential African-American educator, urged industrialists to hire black people "whose habits you know...whose fidelity and love you have tested... [and] who shall stand by you with a devotion that no foreigner can approach." He urged the business leaders not to "look to the incoming of those of foreign birth and strange tongue and habits" for their workforce needs.

Today African Americans continue to suffer from the effects of immigration. Most immigrants live in metropolitan areas, such as New York, Los Angeles, Chicago, San Francisco, Miami, Houston, San Diego, and Philadelphia. More than 93 percent of immigrants settle in metropolitan areas. It is precisely these areas where large African-American populations live. The immigrants have competed with African Americans for jobs in these areas. According to economist Vernon M. Briggs, Jr., "The mass entry of immigrants into these central cities has increased the competition for available jobs. Under these conditions, an inordinate [unduly high] number of black males have despaired of seeking work in the regular economy."

In recent years, large numbers of African Americans have lost their jobs and have been displaced by Mexican Americans, such as in the building maintenance industry in Los Angeles. In the October 1992 issue of *Atlantic* magazine, writer Jack Miles notes: "The almost total absence of black gardeners, busboys, chambermaids, nannies, janitors and construction workers in a city with a notoriously large pool of unemployed, unskilled black people leaps to the eye...." He adds: "If the Latinos were not around to do that work, non-black employers would be forced to hire blacks—but they'd rather not. They trust Latinos. They fear or disdain blacks. The result is unofficial but widespread preferential hiring of Latinos—the largest affirmative-action program [a program designed primarily to help minorities and women in the areas of education and employment] in the nation, and one paid for, in effect, by blacks."

Today, we continue to admit hundreds of thousands of immigrants who lack education, or who are without any substantial education. Yet these people will compete for unskilled jobs at a time when we are becoming a society with an economy that finds little need for unskilled workers.

Advocates of more immigration argue that immigrants take jobs that natives refuse to do. But there is no evidence to support such a view. American workers are willing to work in mines, factories, and construction projects so long as the pay makes the work worthwhile. Historically, there has been no problem in getting natives to do agricultural work either so long as the pay made such positions suitable to the work. But the agriculture industry relies on foreign workers because it can pay them less than American workers. News stories describe the large number of applicants for jobs—even menial (low-paying, low-skilled) jobs—when a major corporation announces that it is prepared to hire in large numbers. It is obvious that low-skilled workers are willing and able to take jobs under the right economic conditions.

The economic problem for native-born Americans is worsened because of the kinship ties of immigrants. Once immigrants come into a job, they establish ethnic networks to encourage relatives and friends to apply for jobs in the same companies, thus shutting out native workers who do not even hear of job openings.

Public assistance. Like other advanced industrial societies, the United States provides its citizens with a number of public services that are paid in whole or in part from public funds.

In a study reported in 1993, Rice University economist Donald L. Huddle found that the public costs associated with immigrants settling in the United States amounted in 1992 to $42.5 billion more in services and assistance than the $20.2 billion that immigrants paid in taxes.

Peter Brimelow examined the group of immigrants arriving in the five years before 1970. He found: "[W]elfare participation actually increased the longer they were in the United States. Originally, their rate was 5.5 percent; the 1990 Census reported it at 9.8 percent. All waves of immigrants show a similar drift. The conclusion is unavoidable: immigrants are assimilating [adapting] into the welfare system."

It is sometimes said that the welfare gap between welfare received by immigrants and welfare received by native households is caused by refugees

Public schools are required to admit immigrant children, even if they are illegal immigrants.

and/or elderly persons. Using data supplied by the Survey of Income and Program Participation (SIPP), a randomly selected household survey about involvement in nearly all means-tested programs (programs offering benefits to those in financial need), George J. Borjas showed that such a claim is false. Removing from the survey of immigrant households all immigrant households that either originate in countries from which refugees come or that contain any elderly persons, he found: "17.3 percent of this narrowly defined immigrant population receives benefits, v. 13 percent of native households that do not contain any elderly persons. Welfare gap: 4.3 percentage points (proportionately, 33 percent)."

Because immigrants do not settle in the different states of the United States in proportion to the population of those states, the welfare burden is particularly felt in a few areas of the United States. Most immigrants concentrate in six states: California, Texas, Florida, New York, New Jersey, and Illinois. Such concentration places an exceptional burden on the governments of these states because the federal government takes in the bulk of tax money but states pay the bulk of money for services. California has the biggest problem of any state. Between 1975 and April 1994, of the approximately 8.6 million refugees, illegal immigrants, and illegal immigrants granted amnesty under the 1986 IRCA, one-half, or approximately 4.3 million, resided in California. According to Eloise Anderson of the California Department of Social Services, nearly 13 percent of beneficiaries of Aid to Families with Dependent Children (AFDC) in California are refugees or the children of refugees. (AFDC is a program providing financial aid for families of children who lack adequate support but are living with one parent or relative, or in some states, living with both parents where the breadwinner is unemployed.) She adds that 40 percent of all Medi-Cal (the California Medicaid program) births are born to illegal immigrants in California. (Medicaid is a program that provides medical assistance for those people unable to pay for it.)

The cost to California taxpayers for AFDC, SSI, medical care, and general assistance for immigrants was $1 billion in 1994. Added to this figure are California's costs for incarceration (jailing) of illegals of $400 million, and $1.7 billion to educate the children of illegal immigrants. In California, moreover, a third of all public assistance goes to immigrant-headed households.

Illegal immigrants impose a particularly strong burden in the Los Angeles area. A survey by the Los Angeles County Department of Health Services found that nearly two-thirds of all mothers who gave birth in the county's four public hospitals in the 1990–1991 fiscal year (a period equal to a calendar year but beginning on a date other than January 1) were undocumented (illegal immigrants). These illegal immigrant women accounted for an estimated 28,800 births.

Certainly, immigrants pay taxes, but they get more in services than they pay in taxes when the cost of education is included. No doubt the welfare problem would be less than it is if the United States were more selective in the kind of immigrants that it admits—that is to say, emphasizing skills, education, and wealth rather than family ties. In contrast, Canada and Australia benefit by their policies of attracting those who have the most to contribute to their economies.

It is true that the welfare reform law and immigration laws enacted in 1996 will reduce welfare benefits. But both legal and illegal immigrants will still be able to obtain some benefits.

At one time, U.S. immigration policy was driven by economic need and a search for greater economic development. Millions of immigrants—many of whom lacked skills and education—found jobs in the American economy. Today, the United States continues to admit immigrants most of whom are selected on the basis of considerations that have nothing to do with how they may help the U.S. economy. The result is a rising welfare dependency and harm to the American economy.

No. Immigrants are a convenient scapegoat for many of the nation's problems. Particularly during a downturn in the economy, political leaders and writers blame immigrants for contributing to economic decay. But the evidence shows that rather than being a drawback to the economy, they are an asset.

Economic growth. To have growth, a nation needs both workers and capital (wealth, or any form of wealth used to produce more wealth). Historically, the kinds of people who have come to the United States have been young and energetic, eager to find work and build businesses in a land that encouraged economic opportunity. From colonial times to the early 20th century, immigrants rushed to America and contributed mightily to making its agricultural economy rich. As the nation moved from an agricultural to an industrial economy, it drew on still more immigrants to work in its mines, mills, and factories. Immigrants helped build the nation's canals, railroads, and highways.

Because the immigrants who came to America were mostly young, they were not an economic drain on the communities in which they worked. According to Alejandro Portes and Rubén G. Rumbaut in *Immigrant America: A Portrait:* "The available studies coincide on two points: The very poor and the unemployed seldom migrate, either legally or illegally; and unauthorized immigrants tend to have above-average levels of education and occupational skills in comparison with their homeland populations. More important, they are positively self-selected in terms of ambition and willingness to work." It is not surprising that the poorest and oldest do not leave their homelands for another country because they lack both money to make the trip and energy to find a place in a highly competitive economy.

The unlimited supply of immigrant labor meant that employers could always be assured of workers to perform the many tasks of a booming economy. The effect of the large labor supply was to keep production costs down and to make products and services available to the American people at low cost. The standard of living of the American people rose dramatically due in part to the continuing flow of immigrants.

Immigrants contribute to economic development not only as workers but as entrepreneurs, as well. For example, according to the Census Bureau, 15 percent of Greek and 18 percent of Korean immigrants were self-employed in 1990. Sometimes, immigrants enter business because that is one of the few areas open to them. For example, because Asian Americans experienced racial discrimination and working-class opposition in the late 19th and early 20th centuries, many of them became shopkeepers and small businesspeople. At other

Koreans run a large number of greengrocers in New York City.

times, however, immigrants became entrepreneurs because they hungered for the wealth that their business knowledge and hard work could produce.

Today, immigrants are more likely to go into small businesses than people who are citizens. It is not uncommon to find owners of barber shops, convenience stores, and restaurants, who are immigrants. Taxi drivers are often self-employed immigrants, too. As the small businesses of immigrants prosper, they create jobs. According to economist Julian L. Simon, "Several studies show that firms with fewer than 20 employees, which employ about 33 percent of all working persons, create somewhere between 51 and 80 percent of the new jobs. The data for firms with fewer than 100 employees, and those with fewer than 500 employees, show the same high propensity [tendency] to create new jobs."

In the late 20th century, economic development depends to a great extent on intellectual power. Technological advance, which requires the educational talent that a nation can bring to bear in producing goods and services, is a major factor in economic development. U.S. immigration law provides for admitting up to 140,000 highly educated and technologically skilled workers with talents that are in short supply among native citizens. The United States gains from the knowledgeable immigrants who contribute their considerable intellectual resources to their adopted nation. And foreign graduate students in the sciences supply their own ideas, which often result in new discoveries. To the extent that the law encourages skilled people to come and work in the United States, it has a decided advantage in creating wealth and becoming a world leader in many areas. One of the great assets of the high-tech industries is the large number of scientists and engineers from foreign countries who are working in such globally competitive industries as computers, biotechnology (the application of the principles of engineering and technology to the life sciences), and robotics (the use of automatically controlled mechanisms to perform specific, usually complicated and repetitive industrial tasks).

Recent immigrants are coming to the United States with considerable educational resources. Writer Denise M. Topolnicki observes in *Money* magazine that between 1970 and 1990, the educational talent of immigrants actually improved. She writes: "Between 1970 and 1990, the percentage of immigrants with college degrees climbed from 19% to 27%. Meanwhile the portion of immigrants who dropped out of high school fell to 37% from 48%. (By comparison, 15% of native-born Americans are high school dropouts and 27% are college graduates.) Nearly half (47%) of African immigrants hold college degrees."

It is not surprising that immigrants contribute so much to economic development. Immigrants traditionally have been willing to work hard and for low wages because those wages, although low by U.S. standards, are higher than in the country they left. The wage differential between Mexico and the United States shows the largest income gap between any two countries in the world that border on each other. Average U.S. wages are 12 times those of Mexican wages. According to economist Philip L. Martin, the average annual income in the richest 22 countries in 1992 was $22,000. In contrast, in low- and middle-income countries, it was on average $1,000. Martin concludes: "A person in those countries could increase his or her income 22 times by entering the U.S., Germany, or Japan."

Some industries, such as fruit and vegetable farming, are dependent upon foreign workers. Stephen Moore of the Cato Institute, a public-interest research organization, notes that the fruit and vegetable industry in California might not have been able to compete with its counterpart in Mexico were it not for a steady supply of low-paid immigrants. The garment industry has also been dominated by new immigrants for more than a century. The ethnic background of garment workers changed from Irish to Swedish, German, Italian, East European, Puerto Rican, Chinese, Korean, Dominican, and Mexican, but the industry was kept alive by the flow of new immigrants.

The garment industry has been dominated by new immigrants for more than a century.

The immigrant story in America is a great success story from the point of view of economic development. Census Bureau figures for 1990 show that immigrants who arrived in the United States before 1980 actually had higher average household incomes ($40,900) than all native-born Americans ($37,300). Immigrants, then, not only contribute to the nation's economy but share in the benefits that a booming economy bestows upon those who work hard.

Jobs. In bad times, it is always easy to look for villains to explain away conditions that cause people to lose their jobs. Immigrants have always been a popular target for those who do not find a desirable place in the economy. The idea that immigrants hurt the economy by taking jobs away from American citizens ignores the fact that immigrants require services that contribute to the economy. Immigrants take jobs or build businesses. They earn income, which they spend on the same basic items that citizens purchase, such as food, clothing, and housing. When the demand for goods and services increases, the people who are needed to create or provide those goods and services are hired, and their economic situation improves. In this way, immigrants create jobs.

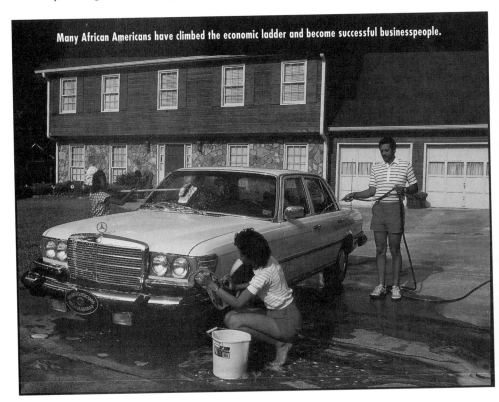

Many African Americans have climbed the economic ladder and become successful businesspeople.

Immigrants are not responsible for unemployment either. Unemployment is caused by changes in the business cycle (upward and downward movements in business activity). In the 19th century, for example, immigration levels declined with the coming of every depression and expanded only when business conditions improved, although the United States had virtually open borders for nearly anyone who wanted to enter. Immigrants came only when the American economy had jobs for them to fill.

It is true that the wage level of immigrants is lower than that of native American citizens. But that is because immigrants are likely to take jobs that are among the lowest paid. In those cases in which immigrants do take jobs from citizens, the displacement results in an upward direction. As historian Maldwyn Allen Jones notes: "Since immigrants tended to gravitate to the lowest rungs of the economic ladder, their coming enabled both the native population and earlier immigrants either to rise to supervisory or managerial positions or to take advantage of the increased opportunities for skilled, professional, and white-collar workers which economic expansion made possible."

Those who see immigration as responsible for the loss of American jobs particularly to African Americans are wrong. Many African Americans have climbed the economic ladder particularly since the enactment of civil rights laws in the 1960s. Those African Americans who have made their way successfully into the American economic system are business and professional people. The fact that African Americans still experience large-scale unemployment and underemployment cannot be denied. But the cause of this situation of economic difficulty can be explained by other factors, such as urban decay, racism, poor schools, and other social and economic factors. Immigrants are not responsible for the plight of unemployed African Americans.

Public assistance. The argument that immigrants require an undue amount of public assistance is a distortion of the facts. The Urban Institute, a research organization in Washington, D.C., examined the economic data and concluded that in 1992, immigrants paid $25 billion to $35 billion more in taxes than they received in public services and assistance. This result is in sharp contrast to the finding of Donald L. Huddle that immigrants accounted for $42.5 billion more in services and assistance than the $20.2 billion that they paid in taxes. George J. Borjas concludes that the net contribution of immigrants was $7 billion.

By law, immigrants must pay income and Social Security taxes, just as nonimmigrants do. They pay other taxes, such as property taxes (either directly through ownership of property or indirectly as part of their rent). They also pay local and state sales taxes. Before 1996, for the first three to five years that they were in the United States, legal immigrants were not eligible for many benefits. With the changes in the 1996 laws, however, they will be eligible for even fewer benefits. Because most immigrants are young, they will be paying money into the welfare system for many years before they can obtain many of the services that government provides, such as Social Security.

The idea that immigrants are an undue burden on the nation's welfare system is based on misleading facts. Refugees rely heavily on welfare because they arrive in the United States with few resources. It is true that 9 percent of immigrant households collect welfare benefits compared to 7 percent of households headed by native-born Americans. But the refugees come largely from war-torn or Communist countries. According to Denise M. Topolnicki, the refugee welfare figures include Cambodia (50 percent of all households), Laos (46 percent), Vietnam (26 percent), the former Soviet Union (17 percent), and Cuba (16 percent). Because refugees are eligible for public assistance as soon as they arrive, there is an unevenness to the welfare figures: 16 percent of the refugees in contrast to only 3 percent of other immigrants who came to the United States during the 1980s received public assistance.

According to the law, refugees may receive benefits from the moment they arrive in the United States, unlike all other immigrants. The elderly also receive a large amount of welfare because many of them have not worked long enough in the United States to receive Social Security and pensions. But as Urban Institute scholars Jeffrey S. Passel and Michael Fix observe: "Welfare use among non-refugee, working-age immigrants (ages 15–64) is extremely low and, contrary to popular perception and some current research, falls well below that of natives. Welfare use among illegal immigrants seems undetectable."

Although newly arriving refugees can get public assistance, they do not stay on public assistance. The Office of Refugee Settlement reported in 1989 that half of the Southeast Asian refugees who arrived in the United States were unemployed at the end of 1985. But that percentage dropped sharply to only 20 percent in 1986, 9 percent in 1987, and 5 percent in 1988. As Stephen Moore notes: "That is, after four years, the 1985 refugees' unemployment rate matched the national rate." And illegal immigrants do not take advantage of most welfare services because they are in fear of being discovered and returned home. Often, they pay taxes but do not receive the public services that are available to citizens.

Most immigrants who come to the United States do not do so for welfare. In fact, nonrefugee immigrants are less likely to be on welfare than native-born

Americans. And as Denise M. Topolnicki observes, immigrant youngsters are not a burden on public education either. She reports in 1995 that only 4 percent of the $227 billion the United States devotes to education is spent educating legal immigrant children and just 2 percent is spent on the estimated 648,000 children who are in the United States illegally.

Immigration critics have made much of the decline in skills of immigrants over time as an explanation for why public assistance costs are increasing. But there really has not been a decline. As Stephen Moore notes: "There has been an improvement in immigrant quality over time, but this improvement simply has not kept pace with the improvements in education and skills of U.S.-born workers."

Immigrants in America are a continuing success story in many ways, not least of which is in helping to expand the U.S. economy. One should not be surprised that immigrants are now succeeding in the United States because they have been succeeding for centuries. It would be counterproductive for the United States to abandon such a rich resource that furnishes so many rewards not only for immigrants but for native-born Americans, as well.

Chapter 6

IMMIGRATION AND PUBLIC ASSISTANCE

Debate: Should Public Assistance Other Than Emergency Medical Care Be Denied to Illegal Immigrants?

Among the issues that divide Americans, few produce as much con-troversy as the giving of public assistance to people who receive such aid. The term welfare is broadly used to describe government programs for people in need, such as the elderly, disabled, and poor, as well as those who are unable to find jobs. In the 20th century, the idea that government is the provider and protector of individual security and social good is widely accepted in most modern govern-ments; and the term welfare state has been used to describe a country that provides government services to fulfill these purposes.

Today as in the past, however, the welfare state has its critics. The chief criticism comes from those who argue that government is a problem and not a solution. They say that when government takes responsibility for solving people's problems, it funds these solutions by taking money from people who have it and giving it to people who do not. The result is to reduce an individual's control over his or her own wealth and to discourage people of talent and accom-plishment from working harder for fear that a good share of their earned income will be taken from them in the form of taxes. Still others complain that when government provides benefits to people, they become dependent upon government and then have no or little incentive to work or to get out of their bad situation.

The attack on the welfare state has been particularly strong in the United States since the election of Ronald Reagan as President in 1980. It grew in strength in the 1990s. Federal, state, and local governments have not by any means destroyed the welfare state, but they have cut back on the benefits that they used to give. In reducing the levels of government spending in many welfare programs, governments at all levels have attempted to make certain that welfare goes to those in need rather than those who are able to work or survive without receiving government benefits.

As part of the overall rethinking about welfare, political officials and interest group leaders have focused attention on the role of immigrants in the welfare state. The welfare reform law and the immigration reform laws of 1996 tightened up public assistance benefits to legal and illegal immigrants. (See Chapter 8.) But immigrants still receive public assistance in one form or another. Refugees, for example, still get SSI and food stamp benefits. Although illegal immigrants are not eligible for most welfare, they are eligible for emergency medical care. In addition, when a child of illegal immigrants is born in the United States, he or she is automatically entitled to social benefit programs. This is so because the Fourteenth Amendment to the Constitution states that all persons born in the United States "are citizens of the United States and of the State wherein they reside."

Immigrants—even if they are undocumented—also benefit from a free public education, just as do all U.S. citizens. In 1982, the Supreme Court ruled in *Plyler v. Doe* that states may not deny children access to public elementary and secondary education on the basis of their status as aliens. The Supreme Court overturned a Texas law barring illegal aliens from public schools. Finally, some illegal immigrants use false identification papers to obtain welfare benefits, such as food stamps, to which they are not entitled. Law-enforcement agencies have attempted to go after those who falsely get such benefits.

Among state governments, California has sought to place the greatest restrictions on furnishing welfare benefits to illegal immigrants. In 1994, critics of illegal immigration in California succeeded in getting enough signatures to place on the ballot what became known as the "Save Our State" initiative. An initiative is a political means allowing voters directly to propose legislation or constitution-

Authors of Proposition 187, Ron Price and Barbara Coe, address supporters of the initiative on November 8, 1994, at a Republican election night party in Costa Mesa, California.

al amendments. Known as Proposition 187, the initiative called for a screening system for people seeking tax-supported benefits. According to the wording of Proposition 187, no person, whether a citizen, legal immigrant, or illegal immigrant, "shall receive any public social services to which he or she may otherwise be entitled until the legal status of that person has been verified."

The proposition has five major sections. The first section prevents illegal immigrants from attending California's public education systems from elementary school to universities. Public educational institutions would have to verify the legal status of students and their parents. The second section requires all providers of publicly paid, nonemergency health-care services to verify the legal status of persons seeking services in order to be reimbursed by the state of California. Individuals requiring emergency services would have to establish their legal status, although even undocumented immigrants would be entitled to emergency services. The third section states that anyone requesting cash assistance and other benefits must verify his or her legal status before receiving such benefits. The fourth section requires all the people who provide public services to report suspected aliens to California's attorney general and to the INS. The fifth section makes it a state offense to make, distribute, and use false documents to obtain public benefits or employment by concealing his or her legal status.

Californians voted in favor of the proposition by a nearly 3-2 ratio (59 percent to 41 percent). California Governor Pete Wilson issued an executive order to all affected state offices to draft emergency regulations for implementing Proposition 187. He also suspended prenatal (before birth) health care to illegal immigrants. If implemented, Wilson's order would have meant a cutoff of services, such as blood tests, physician consultations, and after the baby was born, well-baby checkups.

The Los Angeles City Council and school district voted not to enforce Proposition 187. Opponents of Proposition 187 immediately went to court and succeeded in getting the court to issue an injunction (an order prohibiting the carrying out of a law). The injunction also required all health-care institutions and medical offices in the state to post notices that the law is not in effect and care will be provided without the observation of the INS. In November 1995, a federal district judge declared that most of the provisions of the law were in violation of the Constitution of the United States and could not be enforced. The state of California appealed the decision, and the case is expected to go all the way up to the U.S. Supreme Court for final decision.

This chapter uses Proposition 187 to debate the issues involved in considering public assistance to illegal immigrants. It is clear that other proposed legislation raises related but somewhat different issues.

DEBATED:

SHOULD PUBLIC ASSISTANCE OTHER THAN EMERGENCY MEDICAL CARE BE DENIED TO ILLEGAL IMMIGRANTS?

Yes. Immigrants to the United States have made great contributions to the nation and to the states in which they live and work. When they become citizens, they are entitled to the full benefits to which citizens born in the United States are eligible. But U.S. citizens who live, work, and pay taxes have no obligation to provide public assistance to people who are illegally in the United States. That is why Proposition 187 is a good idea for California and, for that matter, for other states.

Cost. The cost of providing public services is enormous. In California, for example, the cost of educating illegals in 1994 was approximately $1.5 billion in state funds. Governor Wilson reports that two-thirds of all babies born in Los Angeles public hospitals are born to illegal immigrants and that 40 percent of the state's Medi-Cal budget is spent on illegal immigrants. California taxpayers are paying $400 million per year to provide medical care to approximately 317,000 illegals. In Los Angeles illegal immigrants number just under 1 million, or one and a half times the population of Washington, D.C. Californians spend $475 million a year to put convicted illegal immigrants into prison and jails. The state of California does not have unlimited funds. Particularly during tough economic times, states have difficulty coming up with money to pay for their legitimate needs.

The nation is experiencing great problems in furnishing the money to provide for public services. Reports show that many public schools are not succeeding in getting students to learn basic skills in reading and mathematics, let alone the more advanced subjects. In addition, public health service providers cannot furnish the care that their clients require because of overcrowding of hospitals and great demands for social services. Overcrowding, caused in part by the large number of illegal immigrants, contributes to the decay in the quality of education and public health services that the states furnish to their legal citizens. States particularly are in financial trouble because the federal government requires states to deliver many public services. In California's case, these requirements, or federal mandates as they are called, amounted to $3 billion a year in 1994, a figure that is almost 10 percent of the state's general-fund budget.

More than 35 million Americans lack health insurance because they cannot afford to pay for it. Many of the uninsured cannot meet the necessary payments for such insurance. The costs are high in part because of the need to provide free health services for the illegal immigrants. If illegal immigrants can no longer obtain these health benefits, then the costs of health insurance will go down, thus making it possible for more people who are not now able to afford health insurance to buy it.

Critics of Governor Wilson claim he was heartless to order the elimination of prenatal assistance for illegal immigrants (an order that was not implemented because of a federal judge's injunction). But what critics ignore is that he asked that all the money saved from the crackdown on illegal immigrants in the Access for Infants and Mothers program state-financed effort be poured back into that program for the benefit of those legally entitled to the benefits. The Access for Infants and Mothers program is a preventive medical program of the state of California for the working poor that helps treat pregnant women and the babies born to them who are just above the poverty line.

Rule of law. Undocumented immigrants are lawbreakers and should be treated accordingly. They are in the United States in violation of the laws. It is bad enough that they are here at all. It is worse that some of them receive public assistance to which they are not entitled. Government has a responsibility to assure that the laws are faithfully carried out. Proposition 187 helps strengthen the rule of law by requiring that only those who are eligible for public benefits get them.

Critics of Proposition 187 say that it is unconstitutional. Among other matters, they point to the Supreme Court decision in *Plyler v. Texas.* This case, however, needs to be reheard in light of changes that have occurred since the Supreme Court made its decision in 1982. In writing for the majority in that case, Justice William Brennan said that denying illegal aliens in Texas free schooling could not be justified as a way to discourage immigration "when compared to the alternative of prohibiting employment of illegal aliens." He added, "Moreover, there was no evidence to indicate that illegal entrants imposed any significant burden on [Texas's] economy." The fact that Congress did not prohibit illegal aliens from gaining employment was viewed as implied approval by Congress to such employment.

But conditions have changed. The illegal immigration problem has become worse, particularly for California. And Congress passed IRCA in 1986, which made it a federal law requiring an employer to hire only those individuals with a legal right to work in the United States. When the Court reconsiders Proposition 187, it will have an opportunity to reverse the earlier decision.

Effectiveness. The opportunity to obtain welfare benefits is an incentive for aliens to come into the United States legally if possible, illegally if necessary. If babies are born to pregnant women—even if they are undocumented—then the mother becomes eligible to receive many welfare benefits for her child. Fraudulent documents allow some illegals to obtain benefits to which they are not legally entitled. And even children of undocumented immigrants are allowed to attend public elementary school and high school at public expense. In some states, they can even pay the same tuition for college and university as in-state citizens.

The welfare benefits that are available in the United States are much higher than the welfare benefits that they can obtain in the countries that are sending so many immigrants to these shores, most notably Mexico and China. It is no wonder, then, that welfare is a magnet drawing so many illegals here. Cut off the welfare benefits, and the number of illegal immigrants in the United States will decline.

Professionalism and privacy. Critics of Proposition 187 say that it will force teachers and doctors to violate their professional responsibilities. It is not true that teachers will become state informers about their students. Teachers would not even be involved in the process of determining legal status. Rather, it would be the work of school administrators, who already have the responsibility for verifying the residence of a child, to ensure that he or she is legally living in the school district and is entitled to study there. Those furnishing medical and health-care services will be required to gather sufficient information about their clients, very much like the other information they obtain about them. Such a procedure would not be an attack on professionalism.

Proposition 187 respects an individual's right to privacy. All that is required is that those government agencies that administer services make sure of legal residency before they furnish those services. This is not a harsh requirement. In fact, in employment, it is already the law of the land. According to IRCA, for example, an employer is required to check on legal residency from new employees. Applicants for medical care in many states must disclose their Social Security number. These are not violations of privacy, and Proposition 187 would not be a violation either.

Critics of Proposition 187 really are not interested in dealing with the problem of illegal immigration. At times, they pay lip service to favoring controls, but they oppose any serious measures that would deal with the problem of controlling illegal immigration. Welfare benefits serve as an attraction that encourages immigration to the United States both for legal and illegal immigrants. The United States simply can no longer afford to pay out so much money if it hopes to meet the needs of the legitimate taxpayers who are in need of public services.

No. Proposition 187 is a cruel measure. If the Supreme Court ever declares it constitutional, it will end almost all the social services that illegal immigrants get, such as child welfare, foster care, nonemergency health care (including prenatal services), and public education for elementary, high school, and university students. The result would not only be disastrous to the beneficiaries of the program but also would produce results that the supporters of the proposition do not intend.

Cost. If Proposition 187 went into effect, the state of California would lose much of its federal assistance. Estimates by a California legislative analyst calculate that lost aid to schools, public hospitals, and clinics could add up to $15 billion a year. According to a *Los Angeles Times* estimate, if illegal immigrants pulled their noncitizen children out of public schools, that development could cost the state $2.8 billion of federal education aid each year.

A close look at the particulars of Proposition 187 suggests that rather than reducing public expenditures, the measure would result in the skyrocketing of costs for meeting essential services. If pregnant women cannot obtain health care, a high proportion of children will be born with birth defects and diseases. Studies show that lack of prenatal care is linked to the delivery of premature and underweight babies, children with learning disorders, and even fetal alcohol syndrome (birth defects that occur in infants born to alcoholic mothers). Emergency costs would rise from having to deal with health problems in most cases for the lifetime of the child and the mother. People in need of other medical care will avoid treatment for fear of being reported to the INS by health and medical officials, possibly leading to deportation. Later, their medical condition will worsen, and the costs of emergency care will increase accordingly.

In addition, a system of checking the legal status of students and applicants for social services would require the efforts of a large number of government administrators and inspectors. In other words, taxpayers would be faced with yet another big government program, which would require tax money to fund. Taxpayers will find the administrative costs of such a program to be excessive.

Rule of law. The courts have held that even undocumented immigrants have rights in the United States. The right to public education for children who are illegals is a good example and should remain the practice. The circumstances surrounding the *Plyler* decision in 1982 were the same as they are in the late 1990s. In 1982, Texas had an illegal immigration problem and a high proportion of Mexican students (many of them illegals) in Texas districts along the Texas-Mexico border. California today has an illegal immigration problem and a high proportion of Mexican students (many of them illegals). The arguments made by the Texas attorney general about the financial burden and low quality of education are similar to those made by the supporters of Proposition 187.

But the Supreme Court correctly did not accept Texas's case. Speaking for the majority, Justice Brennan stated that although illegals can be denied state benefits, "children...can affect neither their own conduct nor their own status."

He added: "[V]isiting condemnation on...an infant...is contrary to the basic concept of our system that legal burdens should bear some relationship to individual responsibility or wrongdoing.... Penalizing [them for] a legal characteristic over which children can have little control...is an ineffectual—as well as unjust—way of deterring the parent."

Brennan also noted the major role that education plays in society "in sustaining our political and cultural heritage, ...[its] fundamental role in maintaining the fabric of our society." He pointed out the consequences to children that not knowing how to read or write would make youngsters unable "to absorb the values and skills on which our social order rests."

The rule of law will be maintained by getting rid of Proposition 187 in another way: by recognizing the appropriate role of the federal government. Immigration is a federal and not a state problem. Already the federal district court judge has thrown out some of the provisions of Proposition 187 on the grounds that the federal government and not the states have responsibility for immigration matters.

Effectiveness. The purpose of Proposition 187 is to make illegals want to go home. That purpose is based on false assumptions. First, most undocumented immigrants do not come to the United States because of the welfare benefits that are offered. They come to work and find jobs. The way to reduce the flow of illegal immigration may be to reduce the economic incentives, not welfare benefits, to people who need them.

Second, no amount of reduction of welfare benefits will make a difference in the decisions that aliens make to come to the United States. The illegal aliens who come to the United States leave their country and in many cases their relatives and friends to come to a new land in which many of them have no or little knowledge of even the English language. In their home countries, they find life miserable. They are willing to endure the greatest of risks—to their health and their life—to make their journey to the United States. So even the misery that would befall them in the United States would be less than the misery that they have left behind.

The health consequences of Proposition 187 would be devastating. Pregnant women would not be eligible for prenatal care. In addition, people with communicable diseases would not be able to get medical attention. Communicable diseases know no boundaries. If people with a disease such as tuberculosis are not able to get treatment, the disease will spread to the rest of the population. It is no wonder that the major medical and health organizations condemned Proposition 187. These included the American Medical Association, the California Medical Association, and the American Public Health Association.

Health officials report that significant immigration-related public health threats include many illnesses, such as malaria, tuberculosis, and viral hepatitis. The most active cases of tuberculosis in Los Angeles County and New York City, the two leading areas of the United States for this disease, are among immigrants. It is important to treat people with infectious diseases. Dr. Marcelle Layton, assistant commissioner for the New York City Department of Health's Bureau of Communicable Diseases, says: "The fact that these people [immigrants] may not have access to health care means it's less likely things of infectious nature will be identified and treated early, before [those infected] become a risk to others." Illegal immigrants with communicable diseases would only spread those diseases to others, including native-born Americans, thus raising public health care costs.

If children are not able to go to public schools, they will probably not attend any schools and will remain uneducated and unable to become part of the social fabric, just as Justice Brennan indicated. Uneducated, they will not be pre-pared to find jobs that are required for a modern economy that depends on an educated workforce. Uneducated people are more likely to become involved in street crime than edu-cated people, so no doubt many will join gangs and wind up in prison. Many law-enforcement offi-cials understand this prospect, and they campaigned against Proposition 187.

One can only wonder what the values of the supporters of Prop-osition 187 are. As Brian O'Leary Bennett, a former chief of staff to Representative Robert Dornan, notes: "Even the worst thugs housed in our prisons get vaccina-tions." And as an editorial in the New York Times (November 24, 1994) asks: "Did Californians really want the people who run child-welfare agencies to abandon child-ren already abandoned by their parents, or to evict abused children now in foster care?"

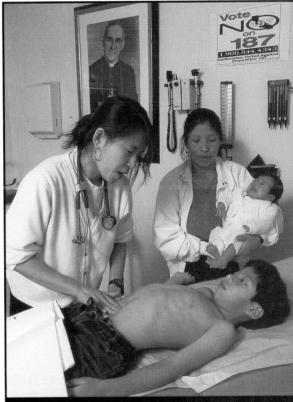

If Proposition 187 were declared constitutional, illegal immigrants would be denied many social services, such as nonemergency health care.

Professionalism and privacy. The effect of Proposition 187 would be to turn school districts into spies for the government. Schools would have to devote their resources to doing the work of the INS rather than the work of educa-tion. Worse, U.S.-born children of illegals may be placed in a position in which, in effect, they will be required to inform on their parents, who may then face deportation.

The law would turn out to be racially discriminatory. No doubt Hispanic and Asian people will more likely be asked to prove their status to live and work in the United States than, say, people who have other racial features, because so many of the undocumented immigrants are of the same heritage. People with names like Sanchez and Lee are more likely to be checked than people who have names like Jones and Smith.

Medical officials have noted that California would lose billions of dollars of federal funding for medical programs because the law would violate confidentiality requirements that are a condition of receiving such funding. One wonders how much further government will go in turning professional health-care providers into law-enforcement officials. Writing in the *New England Journal of Medicine*, Tal Ann Ziv and Bernard Lo ask: "If physicians report illegal immigrants to help enforce the law and balance the state budget, why not also identify tax evaders, traffic-ticket scofflaws, or parents who fail to pay child support?"

Illegal immigration is a problem. But there are many ways to deal with it, such as controlling the borders, speeding up the deportation process, and punishing people who trade in producing fraudulent immigration and identification documents. But the harshest provisions of Proposition 187 that would have such a damaging effect on young and sick people are not only morally unacceptable but are also ineffective in achieving the results that their supporters claim.

Chapter 7
IMMIGRATION AND ASSIMILATION

Debate: Do English Only Laws Serve the Interests of Immigrants?

On a first trip to these shores in search of the "real America," foreign visitors to the United States are sometimes surprised to discover that much of the "real America" is, well, "foreign." As they travel around the country, they see Chinese Americans in Chinatown in San Francisco, Korean Americans in Koreatown in Los Angeles, Italian Americans in Little Italy in Manhattan, and Cuban Americans in Little Havana in Miami. They come upon communities with a heritage from foreign countries, such as cultures from France (Louisiana), Scandinavia (Minnesota), Mexico (Texas), Ireland (Massachusetts), and Germany (Pennsylvania). They also meet descendants of former slaves from Africa and the Caribbean, many of whom live in the nation's big cities.

Most of the people who have come from foreign countries and have settled here permanently have adopted not only a new country but a new culture—an American culture—as well. Culture is the ideas, beliefs, institutions, and language of a community. A remarkable feature of American history is that people from many cultures have come to the United States and embraced American culture. The process by which a group from one culture adopts another culture is known as assimilation. The idea of the melting pot in which racial, cultural, and ethnic groups would assimilate to form a vigorous national society is a popular element of assimilation. The term melting pot was coined by Israel Zangwill, an immigrant, in 1908 in his play, *The Melting Pot.*

Although they become Americans and show loyalty to the laws and practices of the United States, assimilated immigrants and their descendants often keep ties to their native cultures by joining private associations composed of members with similar ethnic, racial, or national origins and even by speaking their native languages. Assimilation has not always been easy in the United States in part because of strong economic, political, and religious differences between immigrants from one country and immigrants from other countries, and between immigrants and people who are native-born Americans. Citizens—some of whom themselves were immigrants or who were first generation native-born—developed unflattering

Visitors to the United States may be surprised to see so many ethnic neighborhoods.

stereotypes (oversimplified images portraying individuals belonging to a group as lacking any individuality) of the new immigrants who were "different from us" because of the clothes they wore, the religion they practiced, the racial features they had from birth, the limited amount of money they earned, and the language they spoke. For example, Chinese who came to the United States in the 19th century were stereotyped as "coolies"—unfree laborers who had been kidnapped or forced into service and shipped to a foreign country. The reality is that they came as free laborers, most of whom borrowed money to make the trip across the Pacific.

Nativists regarded the Chinese as ignorant although China had a superior culture and civilization a thousand years before Christ. It had pioneered in inventions. According to economist Thomas Sowell: "As late as the sixteenth century, China had the highest standard of living in the world." The stereotypes helped produce grim harm to the Chinese immigrants. In the 19th century, Chinese-American homes were burned. At times, gangs killed Chinese people. In Los Angeles in 1871, a mob of white people killed about 20 Chinese in one night.

With the easing of discrimination, Chinese earned professional degrees and by 1959, the average income of Chinese Americans was higher than that of other Americans. They have good jobs and high occupational status today.

Immigrants have been able to assimilate into the U.S. economy by adapting to the needs of that economy. But assimilation also means communicating with people from different groups and cultures who live in the same community. Language is a means of communication by which people talk and listen to each other. If people are monolingual (speak and understand one language), they will not be able to communicate with people who do not speak the same language. Most Americans are monolingual and speak only English. Some are monolingual and speak a language other than English, such as Spanish or Chinese. Some are bilingual (speak two languages) or multilingual (speak many languages). Today, as in the past, some

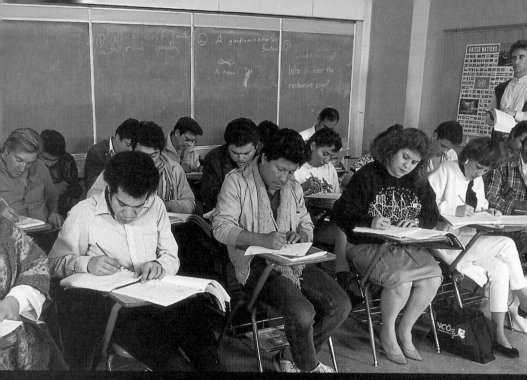

Many immigrants enroll in classes that teach them English so they can better assimilate into the United States.

immigrants to the United States arrive and avoid learning English, preferring to speak their native language in a community of immigrants where a language other than English is commonly spoken.

Some native-born Americans are troubled when immigrants speak a language other than English. Even Benjamin Franklin, who played an important role in the colonial period of American history, feared in 1753 that so many people in his own colony of Pennsylvania spoke German that the legislature would need interpreters. He complained later that many street signs in Philadelphia were written in German.

The belief that people who come to the United States should speak English is a commonly accepted idea of native-born and naturalized Americans. It is an idea that is expressed most prominently when large numbers of non-English-speaking immigrants come to the United States in a relatively short period of time. When the Third

Wave of immigrants came to the United States from East Europe and South Europe between the 1880s and 1914, nativist groups felt that these people were illiterate (could not read or write) because they were unable to communicate in English. Many were able to read and write in their native language, however. Often the nativists argued that speaking in a foreign language was evidence of low intelligence. As a response to nativist criticisms, Congress adopted a law in 1906 requiring an understanding of English in order for a person to become a naturalized U.S. citizen. That requirement remains to this day.

During wartime, Americans have regarded a particular foreign language, notably the language of the nation's enemy, as especially offensive. When the United States entered World War I against Germany in 1917, many Americans were suspicious of German-speaking people. During and after the war, some states even prohibited the teaching of German in public schools because of popular anger against the wartime enemy.

Language again became an issue in American politics after Congress passed an immigration law in 1965, which brought a new wave of immigrants to the country. Because most of these immigrants came from Latin America, the Caribbean, and Asia, many could not speak English when they arrived. The public schools—particularly in California and the Southwest—faced the problem of teaching large numbers of children who spoke and understood a language other than English. Even children of illegal immigrants attended the public schools, a requirement made the law of the land by a Supreme Court decision in 1982.

Congress offered assistance to young immigrants for studying English in 1968, when Ralph Yarborough, a U.S. senator from Texas, sponsored the Bilingual Education Amendments of what became a part of the Elementary and Secondary Education Act. For the first year of the program, the law provided $7.5 million, a relatively small amount of money, to start local demonstration bilingual projects. The purpose of the program, which was voluntary, was to offer help to economically disadvantaged Hispanic children through bilingual methods so that the students would learn basic subjects in their native language while they learned English. Federal money for the program increased over the years so that by the early 1990s, the annual federal funding for bilingual programs had reached $750 million. Hispanic groups and individuals were the major force behind bilingualism. When the bilingual program began, 80 percent of the limited-English schoolchildren in the United States were Spanish speakers.

The federal government's involvement in language education broadened. In 1970, the Office of Civil Rights in the U.S. Department of Health, Education and Welfare issued guidelines for school districts that enrolled more than 5 percent Hispanic or other national-origin minority groups. These guidelines called for the school districts to take steps to help non-English-speaking children to participate in these language programs. These guidelines were compulsory (required) for school districts having even a small percentage of non-English-speaking students if these districts were to receive any federal funds.

In 1974, the Supreme Court decided in *Lau v. Nichols* that school districts should take steps to ensure that non-English-speaking children can participate meaningfully in the educational system. It left to individual school districts the responsibility for working out specific methods for teaching English to non-English-speaking children in accord with regulations of the U.S. Department of Health, Education and Welfare.

Once it was established that public schools must teach foreign-language students, conflict arose about the way in which English was to be taught. Some people said that the most important goal was for youngsters to learn English as quickly as possible. Others said the goal to learn English should not interfere with the use of students' native languages. In this latter view, students should become bilingual rather than monolingual.

Concern about the future of English in America resulted in what has become known as a movement for "Official English" or "English Only." In 1981, S.I. Hayakawa, a U.S. senator from California and himself an immigrant and a linguist, introduced an amendment to the U.S. Constitution that would make English the official language of the United States. Although the United States government conducts its business in English, it does not have an official language, unlike many other countries. The Constitution of the United States does not even mention an official language. In 1983, Hayakawa and Dr. John Tanton, a Michigan eye doctor, created an organization called U.S. English, which sought to promote English as the official language and to encourage the teaching of English in the schools. Other organizations, such as English Only, have also formed to promote similar goals.

Official English means that English should be used for official government functions as determined by law. The adoption of Official English by the federal government might mean that all federal government documents be written in English or that legislative meetings be conducted in English. But Congress could determine that foreign languages be used for some public purposes, such as having legislative deliberations published not only in English but also translated into foreign languages. Some in the English Only movement favor far more demands on government and society to speak English, such as requiring people in the United States to speak English in public places.

By the mid-1980s, U.S. English had become the major organization calling for making English the official language of the United States. It successfully sponsored laws, mostly through referenda (measures passed into law by a popular vote) in states and cities making English the official state and local language. By 1996, 23 states had made English their official language. These laws vary from state to state. The Arizona law, for example, makes English the official language of the state and forces state employees to conduct business in English. The Arizona law does, however, provide for exceptions for non-English languages in order to protect the rights of criminal defendants and victims of crime. The Virginia law is much weaker than the Arizona law. It declares English to be the official language of the state, but it does not prohibit public employees from distributing information in other languages.

U.S. English encouraged the enactment of a federal law making English the official U.S. language, but the law has not been enacted. U.S. English favored expanded opportunities to learn English quickly in schools and at work. It supported legislation on a state and local basis forbidding state or local employees from speaking in a foreign language while working at their government jobs. It opposed the use of the Spanish language, even for government-furnished emergency services in Miami.

The English Only movement has itself produced a response. Organizations have been formed to fight it, most notably the English Plus Information Clearing House (EPIC). Founded in 1987, EPIC is a coalition of 56 groups established under the guidance of the National Immigration, Refugee and Citizenship Forum and Joint National Committee for Languages. It calls for the study of English plus mastery of a second or more languages. It favors classes and programs to promote instruction in English and other languages.

DEBATED:

DO ENGLISH ONLY LAWS SERVE THE INTERESTS OF IMMIGRANTS?

Yes. At a time in which large numbers of immigrants are arriving in the United States, it is important for them to speak English, the language of most Americans. Bilingualism is not the answer to learning English. English Only laws are a good idea. The evidence shows: (1) Bilingualism interferes with the learning of English. (2) Bilingualism is divisive and undermines the feeling that immigrants are part of one people rather than a narrow group, thus hurting immigrants. (3) English Only offers practical solutions to benefit immigrants. And (4) English Only shows respect for different cultures and ethnic groups. Bilingualism—and not English Only—supports public policies that are racist and encourage discriminatory practices.

Bilingualism and English. Although educators promoting bilingual classes claim that their programs are transitional (that is, serve as a step between one stage and another—in this case allowing students to change from speaking only their native language to speaking both their native language and English), the classes rarely make the study of English their primary goal. The people who teach these classes as well as many of their students, mostly Hispanics and Asians, are willing to preserve diverse cultures and traditions even at the expense of undermining an understanding of English.

Independent studies of bilingual programs show their weakness in teaching English. For example, the American Institutes for Research (AIR) made the first comprehensive evaluation of federally funded bilingual programs and concluded in 1977–1978 that they were largely ineffective in teaching English, teaching subjects in a language other than English so that non-

English-speaking students could keep up with English-speaking students, or improving students' sense of self-esteem. This view is shared by experts in bilingualism. Rosalie Pedalino Porter, director of the Bilingual and English as a Second Language program in Newton, Massachusetts, public schools, writes in her book, *Forked Tongue: The Politics of Bilingual Education*, "There is as yet no reliable body of research persuasively supporting the claim that subject matter is better learned in the native language while a student is learning a second language."

Bilingualism is a new development coming out of the 1960s and reverses a traditional practice that immigrants used to learn English. For most of American history, immigrants learned English the old-fashioned way, by taking classes with English-speaking students. They did not need bilingual programs but learned English at school or even at their workplace. And some immigrants learned English in classes for which they paid, mostly at night after work.

The case against bilingualism in schools is not an argument against understanding a foreign language. As the late S.I. Hayakawa observed, the problem is not with bilingualism as such. In his view, bilingual programs are good—but only if their goal is to teach immigrant children to learn English. Specifically, he (and others) recognized that in bilingual programs students are taught subjects, such as mathematics, history, and science, in their native language rather than English, with English being taught only as a separate subject. In Hayakawa's opinion, "The problem with this method is that there is no objective way to measure whether a child has learned enough English to be placed in classes where academic instruction is entirely in English. As a result, some children have been kept in native language classes for six years."

Adopting English Only is not only important for students in school; it has value outside of the classroom, such as in political and governmental matters. When laws exist requiring bilingualism in voting, election information, or other government matters, then the government sends a message: "You don't have to know English to live in America." That is a bad message to send to immigrants and prevents immigrants from assimilating into American society. To the extent that immigrants accept this message, they will not learn English. People who cannot speak English lack the information necessary to participate in the political process and will be uninformed about issues. They will be unable to exercise intelligent and independent judgment on important political matters. Without such information, they rely on "interpreters" who often have a special interest in strengthening minority voting blocs rather than serving the interests of individual immigrants.

The movement to accommodate immigrants by encouraging knowledge of languages other than English makes the administration of public services a great problem for states. For example, Massachusetts offers drivers' tests in 24 foreign languages, including Farsi, Turkish, and Czech. INS tax forms are printed in Spanish as well as in English. It is an administrative and financial burden on taxpayers for such extraordinary attention to be given to non-English-speaking people. As in the past, immigrants ought to learn English and in so doing become part of the assimilation process. Government should do everything within its power to help immigrants, which it does when it creates incentives for immigrants to learn English.

Bilingualism and assimilation. In many cases, bilingualism has become not a movement to promote the speaking of two languages but rather a movement to promote a foreign language instead of English. Bilingualism offers an opportunity for teachers to instill the language and culture of another country. When teachers insist on using Spanish to Hispanic children over a long period of time, as is often the case in bilingual programs, the students learn the values of their native culture at the expense of the values of the United States. The effect is to strengthen the *pluribus*, rather than the *unum* from the *e pluribus unum* (one out of many), which appears on the Great Seal of the United States and is a symbol of national unity. Linda Chavez, the former high-ranking official in the administration of Ronald Reagan and a former president of U.S. English, observes that the purpose of the bilingual amendments of the federal bilingual program has changed "from that of providing remedial help for disadvantaged Hispanic children to that of fostering ethnic identity and group pride." She notes that the effect of promoting another culture at the expense of an American culture has bad consequences for the very people the bilingual program is supposed to help, namely Hispanic and other immigrant young people. She writes: "In the process, these children have become the most segregated students in American public schools, kept apart from their English-speaking peers even after they have acquired basic English skills, sometimes for years."

The experience of nations in which communities speak languages that their fellow citizens do not speak tells us much about what our destiny will be if we continue to undermine English as our national language. In some countries, language is a source of conflict. For example, Belgium, which has language differences between its Dutch- and French-speaking citizens, has experienced political instability. In Canada, nearly half the people of French Quebec want now to secede (separate) from Canada and form an independent country. In recent years, ethnic tensions have torn apart many countries, such as Sri Lanka, Ethiopia, Indonesia, Iraq, Lebanon, Israel, Nigeria, Liberia, Angola, Sudan, Zaire, and Cyprus. Even France, Spain, and Turkey have experienced conflict from ethnic divisions, as expressed by the forces of secessionism by Corsicans (France), Basques (Spain), and Kurds (Turkey). The speaking of different languages and the emphasis on different cultures in the same country can promote the forces that divide rather than unite a people and can lead to political unrest, intergroup killings, and even civil war.

Today the United States can face a similar situation. In the past, immigrants could easily be assimilated into American society through learning English, but assimilation may now be replaced by ethnic and racial group loyalties at the expense of national loyalties to the extent that Hispanic children learn Spanish, Haitian children learn Creole, or African-American children learn "Black English." (Black English is a dialect spoken by many African Americans consisting of English vocabulary and African syntax [the way in which phrases and sentences are formed].)

What has kept the United States from falling apart from the ethnic conflict that so many other countries have experienced is that America's immigrants have been willing to identify with their new nation, the United States. They have adopted the culture and practices of the new land. "The point of America was not to preserve old cultures, but to forge a new American culture," writes historian Arthur M. Schlesinger, Jr.

Some supporters of bilingualism say that English is not the only bond that unites a people. Of course, attachment to the culture and laws of a system is important, too, in creating a sense of American identity. But as S.I. Hayakawa notes: "[I]t is English, our common language, that enables us to discuss our views and allows [us] to maintain a well-informed electorate, the cornerstone of democratic government." The unity of our people requires strengthening the use of English by all people who are members of the American political community.

Practical policy. Like native-born American citizens, immigrants are smart enough to succeed in the United States. Their success depends to a considerable degree on how quickly they can assimilate into American society. An understanding of English is necessary for assimilation.

Immigrant youngsters can learn English properly if they are placed in classes in which they are taught English as quickly as possible, instead of remaining in bilingual classes that delay their learning English. It is true that learning a language is not easy, but today young people receive all kinds of assistance in the schools that earlier generations of immigrant children did not get, such as teachers who are trained to help students with little or poor ability to speak English. Older immigrants, too, can become assimilated to the extent that they master English. To do that, however, means that they must be encouraged to speak in the language of their adopted country as quickly as possible. English Only laws offer practical solutions that can only serve the best interests of immigrants.

Respect for cultural differences. Throughout most of American history, immigrants to the United States were able to show their affection for their immigrant heritage in many different private ways. They formed or joined ethnic associations and established private classes so that their children could appreciate and learn the heritage of their parents. English Only supporters do not seek to ban the private speaking of languages other than English. What they want to do is to encourage immigrants to understand English as quickly as possible and not to be hurt by ignorance of the language of the dominant majority of people who live in the United States.

From a practical perspective, many of the laws requiring respect for other cultures through requirements of bilingualism are themselves racist. For example, the 1975 Voting Rights Amendments to the Voting Rights Act require bilingual ballots for members of selected groups, specifically Asian Americans (Chinese, Filipino, Japanese, and Korean), American Indians, Alaskan natives, and Hispanic people. There are, however, other foreign-language groups in the United States that are not included, such as French-speaking Americans. S. I. Hayakawa correctly notes that according to these amendments, brown people, red people, and yellow people are "assumed not to be smart enough to learn English." That is an assumption that is profoundly racist because millions of people of color have come to the United States, learned English, and become part of the melting pot.

Bilingualism encourages the ethnic and racial discrimination against immigrants that advocates of its philosophy are presumed to oppose. Because bilingual programs slow down the rate at which immigrants learn English, these immigrants are unable to compete effectively in the American economy. According to Linda Chavez: "Most Latin immigrants, especially Mexicans, are poorly educated by U.S. standards and face years of sub-standard wages in the U.S. labor market." Bilingual advocates hurt the cause of immigrants when they force immigrants to keep their native languages. In the name of cultural pride, they leave immigrants unable to compete in the economy and move up the economic ladder, as immigrants in older generations used to do in the United States.

An understanding of English is necessary for immigrants to the United States to become equal members of the American community. Immigrants can and should respect their cultural heritage. But they can do so at the same time that they learn English and benefit from the knowledge of English that people in the American community gain.

No.
Immigrants who come to the United States appreciate the opportunities that their new nation gives to them. They want to become assimilated into their new culture. But English Only laws will not help them, nor will the efforts to destroy bilingual programs. The record of immigration in recent years shows: (1) Bilingualism helps immigrants understand English. (2) Language differences are not the cause of conflict. (3) Official language laws do not promote English. (4) English Only shows disrespect for different cultures and ethnic groups. Its approach is racist and discriminatory.

Bilingualism and English. Bilingualism means knowing two languages, not one. Those who favor English Only often claim that bilingualism means that immigrants will learn only a language other than English. But that claim is not true. Most bilingual teachers want people to understand not only English but another language, as well.

The English Only movement sees a crisis in learning English where a crisis does not even exist. Scholars have shown that historically in the United States, there is a three-generation pattern among non-English-speaking immigrants and their descendants in learning English. The non-English-speaking immigrant generation tends to be monolingual in its native tongue and may know only a limited amount of English. But its children are bilingual, speaking both the language of their parents and English. The third generation may speak only English or at least prefer to speak English.

This pattern continues today as most immigrants understand the importance of learning English in adjusting to life in the United States. To some observers, it appears that the use of Spanish is increasing, but that is because the size of the Spanish-speaking population has been growing. If Hispanic immigration to the United States stopped today, the Spanish language would decline rapidly in usage. A Rand Corporation study of 1985 found that "more than 95 percent of first-generation Mexican Americans born in the United States are proficient [capable of understanding and using] in English and that more than half the second generation speaks no Spanish at all." Today, approximately 95 percent of the American people speak English. English is the language of business across national borders, moreover, so there is every practical economic reason to learn English. And immigrants are practical people.

In 1986, when Proposition 63—the initiative declaring English as California's official language—was being passed, more than 40,000 immigrant adults were being turned away from English as a second language (ESL) classes in the Los Angeles Unified School District alone. In other words, the demand for learning English was far greater than the classes could supply. The demand to study English continues.

Advocates of English Only have a bigger agenda than promoting English. The evidence shows that immigrants recognize that they and their children need to know English in their adopted country. By denying information on voting in a language that people can understand, they are discouraging immigrants from voting, understanding political issues, and otherwise participating in the American political process. When a group of people are systematically excluded from such participation, then government need no longer take their interests into account in making laws. In practical terms, the result is as discriminatory as denying people the right to participate in the political process because of their race or religion.

The view that people who speak Spanish or other foreign language lack necessary information to participate in the political process assumes that English is the only language by which they keep informed about political issues in the United States. But foreign-language newspapers in just about every language imaginable contain stories dealing with political issues. Even the *Miami Herald*, the biggest newspaper in South Florida, has both a Spanish and an English edition, thus allowing non-English-speaking people of Hispanic descent to be informed about issues.

English Only laws can only contribute to a further decline in political participation in the United States that has undermined civic responsibility in the 20th century. The sad fact about voting in the United States is that so few people participate. In presidential elections, only slightly more than one out of two eligible voters casts a ballot. In state and local elections, the turnout is even less. In primaries and referenda, it is usually even lower than in state and local elections. The problem, then, for American society is to encourage political participation and not to set up unnecessary roadblocks to allowing more Americans to participate, as would be the case if the English Only crowd got its way.

Also, the cost of producing driving instructions for non-English-speaking people is not high and is a necessary expense that a caring society must pay. It would be wrong to deny a driver's license to a responsible person

Should the English Only movement be successful, public signs like this one would no longer be commonplace.

merely because that person does not understand English. A responsible non-English-speaking person can tell the difference between red and green lights and can recognize stop signs, let alone read the drawings that often accompany road signs. Finally, responsible people who do not speak English or who have limited understanding of the language earn money and pay taxes. They need help in filling out tax forms, which are often even complicated to Ph.D.s in English literature who are authorities in the English language.

Bilingualism and assimilation. English Only is wrong to look at language as the basis of national unity. Language is not what has united the American people throughout American history. In fact, America has historically been a multilingual country although the dominant language has been English. People of diverse cultures identified with the American nation and sought to become American. It was this desire to identify as Americans, rather than to speak a common language, that was crucial to national unity.

The United States has had a long experience with bilingualism, and there is no evidence that this experience shows that bilingualism has divided people who spoke different languages. Louisiana allowed the publication of its laws, legal notices, and other public documents in French (the language of Cajuns in the southern part of the state) for much of the 19th century. Louisiana courts used both French and English, and every speech of the state legislature was translated. California and Texas also permitted their laws to be published in Spanish, as did New Mexico. Both Spanish and English were the official languages of New Mexico until 1941. Many states, including Louisiana, Minnesota, and Hawaii, allowed for the use of languages other than English for purposes of instruction in some public schools.

Within most countries of the world, people speak different languages, and they get along well in many cases. In Switzerland, for example, many language groups live together peacefully. When conflict occurs among different language groups within a country, the source of the conflict is not usually over a language difference but rather over economic, political, religious, or racial differences.

Speaking a common language means that people can communicate quickly and understand each other instantly without an interpreter on hand. But language is only a means of communication. Language may be looked upon as a messenger that carries words. But it is the message, rather than the character of the messenger, that makes people friendly or hostile. People who speak the same language have been known to go to war against people whose language is the same. The most devastating war of the 19th century was the American Civil War in which Yankees and Southerners fought and died in great numbers. They could understand each other quite well, but they represented forces that differed over issues of slavery and national unity. Similarly, the Irish, who spoke English and were a part of the United Kingdom in the same way that California is part of the United States, fought for independence against the British in the 20th century. In recent years, Serbs and Bosnians both spoke Serbo-Croatian yet fought each other with tragic consequences to human life and property after Yugoslavia broke up in the 1990s. Historically, civil wars and uprisings within nations often have nothing to do with language and everything to do with other matters. So it is wrong to blame language differences for conflict.

If language strengthened cultural conflict in the United States, it would be a threat to national unity. But outside of a few instances in which some political leaders encourage people not to learn English as a requirement of cultural awareness and sensitivity, there is little evidence to show that most programs in bilingualism promote such an attitude. As James C. Stalker notes in an article in *English Journal*: "Multilingualism in a country is potentially dangerous only if it becomes the rallying point for cultural divisiveness. Otherwise, it is a benefit of great economic and political value."

The vision that English Only advocates have is that monolingualism will promote unity. But one has reasonably to ask the question of how the law requiring speaking English would be enforced. Would people be forced to speak English? Would not such a measure create a disunity that the English Only movement claims to want to prevent?

Impractical policy. Even if one favors the speaking of English by new immigrants, writing laws to do so would have the same effect as writing laws to prevent snow or rain. The United States has never had an official language.

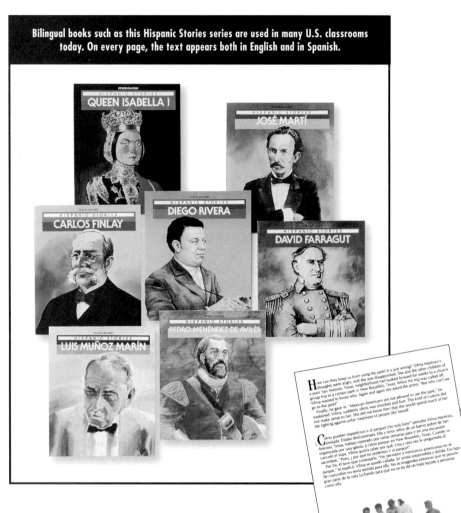

During the Revolutionary War, the Continental Congress, the governing authority of the rebellious Americans in the war against Great Britain, issued official publications in German, French, and English. The Framers of the Constitution never even debated the subject of an official language when they met in Philadelphia in 1787. And yet, millions of non-English-speaking immigrants came to this country and learned English. Even when they did not learn English, their children did, and the grandchildren of the immigrants could not even speak the language of their grandparents in most cases.

Immigrants to the United States are already learning English without benefit of an official English language law. According to social scientist Ben J. Wattenberg: "Hispanics born in the United States or who have been here ten or more years have already reached all U.S. levels in occupation, education, income, and language proficiency." As the saying goes: "If it ain't broke, don't fix it." And the way immigrants are learning English is a system that "ain't broke."

Disrespect for cultural differences. For most of its history, the United States showed a respect for different cultures and recognized linguistic diversity. At the time of the adoption of the Constitution in the late 18th century, the United States was not monolingual. True, most people spoke English, but large numbers of people spoke German or French, and Native Americans spoke hundreds of languages. As the borders of the United States grew as a result of treaties and wars, many Spanish- and French-speaking peoples entered the Union. The naturalized citizens in these territories were not required to demonstrate an understanding of English in order to become citizens. The Framers, the men who wrote the Constitution, did not seek to make English the official language of the United States. English Only laws are an attack on the historic respect that the nation has shown to people who speak languages other than English.

English Only laws are discriminatory in many other ways, too. Passing laws that prohibit the printing of information in foreign languages denies rights to people who need certain kinds of knowledge, such as voting information or emergency and safety literature. Withholding such information is discriminatory and denies people their rights merely because of the language that they speak. As a nation, we reject discrimination because of religious preference, race, age, or physical disability. Similar discrimination directed against non-English-speaking people in this country is equally worthy of rejection because it is a denial of basic rights.

A good deal of the support for English Only comes from people with views that are racist. In a revealing memo meant to be confidential, U.S. English founder John Tanton expressed his concerns in 1988 about the loss of power by the white majority in the United States:

- *Gobernar es poblar* translates "to govern is to populate." In this society where the majority rules, does this hold? Will the present majority peaceably hand over its political power to a group that is simply more fertile?

- Will Latin American migrants bring with them the tradition of the mordida (bribe), the lack of involvement in public affairs, etc.?

• In the California of 2030, the non Hispanic Whites and Asians, will own the property, have the good jobs and education, speak one language and be mostly Protestant and "other." The Blacks and Hispanics will have the poor jobs, will lack education, own little property, speak another language and will be mainly Catholic. Will there be strength in this diversity? Or will this prove a social and political San Andreas Fault [an area in California in which a fracture of the Earth's crust can cause earthquakes when it moves]?

As a result of the memo, Walter Cronkite, the former anchor of CBS News, resigned from his position as a member of the U.S. English advisory board and asked that his name be removed from the organization's letterhead. Linda Chavez, the organization's president, also resigned.

There is nothing new about the discriminatory aspects of movements like English Only. In 1921, Republicans in New York helped pass a law requiring an English literacy test for voting. According to writer James Crawford, they "hoped to disfranchise [deprive a citizen of the right to vote] one million Yiddish speakers who had an annoying habit of electing Democrats." Today, the English Only laws would in effect disfranchise many Hispanics and Asians.

Immigrants have enough problems in coming to a new country and adapting to its ways. Understanding English is a problem. But over time, immigrants and their descendants succeed in learning the language of their adopted country. There is no reason to put new roadblocks in the way of immigrants, as the English Only groups would do.

Chapter 8

CONCLUSION: THE FUTURE OF IMMIGRATION

In the late 20th century, immigration remains a controversial topic. Attempts to adopt new laws dealing with both legal and illegal immigration will no doubt continue to be made in spite of the fact that in 1996, President Clinton signed two laws that are expected to have great influence on immigrants. One law dealt with welfare reform in general, and the other focused entirely on immigration. Both measures resulted from compromises that were made to assure passage in both chambers of Congress as well as win the approval of the President.

The welfare reform law ended the federal government's role in AFDC. Under the new law, the states were given responsibility for dealing with this welfare program. Some of the welfare reform law provisions applied specifically to immigrants. Under these provisions, legal immigrants who were not U.S. citizens would no longer be eligible for most welfare benefits, including food stamps and SSI, during their first five years in the United States. (Exceptions are made for refugees, veterans, and their immediate families.) Refugees who have been in the United States for more than five years will lose assistance. Under the welfare reform law, states would now be allowed to decide whether legal immigrants would be eligible for the Medicaid health-care programs. Legal immigrants, however, continued to be

President Bill Clinton signed the Welfare Bill on August 22, 1996.

eligible for some educational training programs and for Head Start (the federal government's educational program for disadvantaged preschool children).

Although he signed the bill, President Clinton declared that he objected to the provisions denying most welfare benefits to legal immigrants who were not U.S. citizens. In a July 31, 1996 speech, he noted that immigrant families with children who fell on hard times through no fault of their own could have difficulty because they face the same risks the rest of us do from accidents, criminal assaults, and serious illnesses. He added: "They should be eligible for medical and other help when they need it." The President signed the bill because he believed that in spite of its weaknesses, most of the welfare reform measures were needed.

Legal immigrants who could not qualify for most welfare benefits would, however, remain eligible for some others. Among these benefits are emergency Medicaid or state health services, immunizations and testing and treatment of symptoms of communicable diseases (although Medicaid may not fund such immunization, testing, or treatment), short-term noncash, emergency relief, and housing and community development funds.

In May 1997, the Clinton administration and the Republican leadership in the Congress agreed to plan to balance the budget by the year 2002. The plan involved many issues of tax reduction and government spending. One provision of the agreement called for restoring medical and disability benefits for legal immigrants already in the United States. New immigrant arrivals, however, would not be eligible. If Congress and the President cooperate to carry out the plan, then the welfare reform law of 1996 would be revised for the benefit of legal immigrants already in the United States.

The Illegal Immigration Reform and Immigrant Responsibility Act of 1996 dealt mostly with illegal immigrants but did include some items concerning legal immigrants. Specifically, among its main provisions, the law:

- Nearly doubles the size of the Border Patrol by adding 1,000 new agents a year for the next five years.

- Adds 600 new INS investigators to go after illegal immigrants.

- Authorizes $12 million for new border fences and other control measures.

- Increases penalties for alien smuggling and document fraud.

- Establishes voluntary pilot programs in five states with the highest estimated populations of undocumented workers to allow employers to check a government database by computer to verify the work eligibility of job seekers.

- Requires sponsors of immigrant relatives to earn at least 125 percent of the federal poverty level, or find a cosponsor who does to accept joint liability (legal obligation) for the new immigrant.

• Requires the federal government to reimburse hospitals that provide emergency medical services to illegal aliens.

• Tightens up procedures for granting asylum.

• After five years in the United States, allows a legal immigrant to qualify for Medicaid and the other programs only if his or her income, combined with that of his or her sponsor, falls below a certain level.

• Makes it possible for immigrants who receive federal means-tested benefits for more than 12 months during seven years in the United States to be deported.

Some legislators who wanted a stronger bill complained that the bill failed to take effective measures against employers who hired illegal immigrants and did not deal adequately with immigrant misuse of federal and state programs. But other legislators felt that the bill was much too harsh on immigrants.

Certain controversial matters were left out of the new law. Among these were a provision allowing states to end free public education for illegal children and provisions that would have removed some other benefits from aliens. The law weakened the ability of employees to sue for discrimination in the hiring process. And no limits were placed on the number of legal immigrants permitted into the United States.

Many questions remain about the future of immigration. Some states worry about the consequences of the welfare reform legislation. They fear that loss of benefits will undermine their economies. In 1996, California, for example, had nearly 40 percent of the approximately 1.5 million noncitizens who received federal assistance, with most of the rest located in New York, Texas, Florida, and New Jersey. Some immigrants and civil liberties supporters worry about racial discrimination in employment against people who "look foreign." Business and labor groups have their own economic concerns.

In the years ahead, those forces favoring toughening the immigration laws as well as those forces favoring weakening immigration laws will support changes in immigration law. Already, groups opposed to the welfare reform and immigration laws of 1996 are preparing court challenges to those laws on constitutional grounds.

Those on either side of the immigration issue know that the conflict over immigration policy will continue. They understand that historically, the 20th century has many examples of the United States closing and then opening its borders, based on economic, diplomatic, political, and humanitarian considerations. Politics reflects the changing attitudes and interests in society, and one can easily predict that the immigration policy of the United States in the 21st century will be as stormy and controversial as it has been in the 20th century.

ABBREVIATIONS

AFDC	Aid to Families with Dependent Children
AFL	American Federation of Labor
AIR	American Institutes for Research
ATF	Bureau of Alcohol, Tobacco, and Firearms
CIA	Central Intelligence Agency
EPIC	English Plus Information Clearing House
ESL	English as a second language
FBI	Federal Bureau of Investigation
GAO	General Accounting Office
GDP	Gross Domestic Product
INS	Immigration and Naturalization Service
IRCA	Immigration Reform and Control Act
IRS	Internal Revenue Service
LULAC	League of United Latin American Citizens
MALDEF	Mexican American Legal Defense and Education Fund
NCLR	National Council of La Raza
SIPP	Survey of Income and Program Participation

GLOSSARY

affirmative-action programs Programs designed primarily to help minorities and women in the areas of education and employment.

Aid to Families with Dependent Children (AFDC) A program providing financial aid for families of children who lack adequate support but are living with one parent or relative, or in some states, living with both parents where the breadwinner is unemployed.

anarchism A political philosophy that favors the abolition of government.

assimilation The process by which a group from one culture adopts another culture.

asylees People who were already in a foreign country either legally or illegally—unlike refugees—but who, like refugees, sought admission there.

braceros program A program in which Mexican agriculture workers were admitted to the United States to work on farms.

capital Wealth, or any form of wealth used to produce more wealth.

carrying capacity The number of individuals that an area can support without sustaining damage.

census An official count of population.

communism A theory in which private property is eliminated and people own the means of production goods and services being distributed fairly, and with the state playing a minimum role in people's lives.

demographic Population characteristics.

deport To send out of the country by legal means.

disfranchise Deprive a citizen of the right to vote.

displaced persons People who were homeless as a result of World War II.

emigrate To leave a country and live in another country.

ethnic groups People who share common features, such as race, language, and culture.

Fascist A person who favors dictatorial rule and often makes strong appeals to the overwhelming importance of national unity.

fertility The condition of being capable of producing offspring.

gentleman's agreement An understanding by which the parties are bound only by their word of honor.

geothermal energy The Earth's internal heat that is released naturally.

Head Start The federal government's educational program for disadvantaged preschool children.

immigrants People who come to a country to take up permanent residence.

initiative A political means allowing voters directly to propose legislation or constitutional amendments.

isolationism A policy of avoiding entanglements with foreign countries.

Know Nothings People who belonged to secret organizations in the middle of the 19th century, who were anti-Catholic and anti-immigrant.

literacy test An examination requiring a person to prove his or her ability to read and write.

means-tested programs Programs offering benefits to those in financial need.

Medicaid A program that provides medical assistance for those people unable to pay for it.

melting pot A place in which racial, cultural, and ethnic groups would assimilate to form a vigorous national society.

menial Low-paying, low-skilled, usually pertaining to employment.

nativists People who favor native inhabitants rather than immigrants.

naturalized Having become a citizen in a country after immigrating there.

pluralism The condition in which different ethnic and other groups live at peace in a political community.

public charge A person dependent on government assistance to live.

quota system In immigration, a system in which a maximum number of persons is permitted to enter the United States from specific countries per year.

referendum (referenda [pl.]) A measure passed into law by a popular vote.

refugee A person who flees a country usually out of fear of persecution or war.

solar energy Energy produced from the sun.

Supplemental Security Income A public-assistance program for poor people who are elderly, blind, or disabled.

undocumented Illegal (in referring to immigrants).

visas Official authorizations to enter a country.

welfare Government programs for people in need, such as the elderly, disabled, and poor, as well as those who are unable to find jobs.

BIBLIOGRAPHY

Chapter 1: Introduction: A Nation of Immigrants

Daniels, Roger. *Coming to America: A History of Immigration and Ethnicity in American Life*. New York: HarperCollins, 1990.

Handlin, Oscar. *The Uprooted*, 2nd ed. Boston: Little, Brown, 1973.

Jones, Maldwyn Allen. *American Immigration*, 2nd ed. Chicago: University of Chicago Press, 1992.

Kennedy, John F. *A Nation of Immigrants*, rev. ed. New York: Harper & Row, 1986.

Sowell, Thomas. *Ethnic America: A History*. New York: Basic Books, 1981.

Takaki, Ronald. *A Different Mirror: A History of Multicultural America*. Boston: Little, Brown, 1993.

Chapter 2: Immigration and the Law

Bean, Frank D., Barry Edmonston, and Jeffrey S. Passel, ed. *Undocumented Migration to the United States: IRCA and the Experience of the 1980s*. Washington, DC: Urban Institute Press, 1990.

Handlin, Oscar. *A Pictorial History of Immigration*. New York: Crown Publishers, 1972.

Takaki, Ronald. *Strangers from a Different Shore: History of Asian Americans*. Boston: Little, Brown, 1989.

Ungar, Sanford J. *Fresh Blood: The New American Immigrants*. New York: Simon & Schuster, 1995.

Chapter 3: The Immigrant Population

Abernethy, Virginia D. *Population Politics: The Choices That Shape Our Future*. New York: Plenum Press, 1993.

Bouvier, Leon F., and Lindsey Grant. *How Many Americans?: Immigration and the Environment*. San Francisco: Sierra Club Books, 1994.

"In Praise of Huddled Masses." *Wall Street Journal*, July 3, 1984, p. 24.

Myers, Norman, and Julian L. Simon. *Scarcity or Abundance? A Debate on the Environment*. New York: W. W. Norton, 1994.

Ray, Dixie Lee, with Lou Guzzo. *Trashing the Planet: How Science Can Help Us Deal with Acid Rain, Depletion of the Ozone, and Nuclear Waste (Among Other Things)*. Washington, DC: Regnery Gateway, 1990.

Wilson, Pete. "Securing Our Nation's Borders." *Vital Speeches of the Day* 60, no. 17 (June 15, 1994): 534–536.

Chapter 4: Illegal Immigration

Branigan, William. "Influx of Immigrants Meets Beefed-Up Resistance at U.S. Border." *Washington Post*, Feb. 5, 1996, pp. A1, A14.

Cassidy, Peter. "We Have Your Number." *Progressive* 58, no. 12 (Dec. 1994): 28–29.

Glasser, Ira. "No: A Registry Would Create a New Tool for Discrimination." *ABA Journal* 80 (Nov. 1994): 45.

Griffin, Rodman D. "Illegal Immigration." *CQ Researcher* 2, no. 16 (Apr. 24, 1992): 361–384.

Martin, Susan Forbes. "Yes: Technology Can Fight Fraud and Safeguard Privacy." *ABA Journal* 80 (Nov. 1994): 44.

Miller, Alan C. "Data Sheds Heat, Little Light, on Immigration Debate." *Los Angeles Times*, Nov. 21, 1993, pp. A1, A26.

Chapter 5: Immigration and Economic Development

Borjas, George J. *Friends or Strangers: The Impact of Immigrants on the U.S. Economy.* New York: Basic Books, 1990.

————. "Tired, Poor, on Welfare." *National Review* 45, no. 2 (Dec. 13, 1993): 40–42.

————. "The Welfare Magnet." *National Review* 43, no. 4 (Mar. 11, 1996): 48–50.

Briggs, Vernon M., Jr. *Mass Immigration and the National Interest*, 2nd ed. Armonk, NY: M.E. Sharpe, 1996.

Briggs, Vernon M., Jr., and Stephen Moore. *Still an Open Door? U.S. Immigration Policy and the American Economy.* Washington, DC: American University Press, 1994.

Huddle, Donald L. "A Growing Burden." *New York Times*, Sept. 3, 1993, p. A23.

Martin, Philip L. "The Economics of Immigration." *Quill* 83, no. 4 (May 1995): 27–30.

Miles, Jack. "Blacks vs. Browns." *Atlantic* 270, no. 4 (Oct. 1992): 41–45, 48, 50–52, 54–55, 58, 60, 62–65, and 68.

Passel, Jeffrey S., and Michael Fix. "Myths About Immigrants." *Foreign Policy* no. 95 (Summer 1994): 151–160.

Portes, Alejandro, and Rubén G. Rumbaut. *Immigrant America: A Portrait.* Berkeley: University of California Press, 1990.

Simon, Julian L. *The Economic Consequences of Immigration.* Cambridge, MA: B. Blackwell, 1989.

Topolnicki, Denise M. "The Real Immigrant Story: Making It Big in America." *Money* 24, no. 1 (Jan. 1995): 129–131, 133–134, 136–138.

Chapter 6: Immigration and Public Assistance

Chang, Howard F. "Shame on Them, Picking on Children." *Los Angeles Times*, Sept. 6, 1994, p. B5.

"Chasing Immigrants in America." *Wall Street Journal*, Oct. 5, 1994, p. A16.

Ezell, Howard W. "Enough Is More Than Enough." *Los Angeles Times*, Oct. 23, 1994, p. M5.

Herschensohn, Bruce. "Immigration—Draw a Line in California." *Wall Street Journal*, Oct. 26, 1994, p. A20.

Hinojosa, Raul, and Peter Schey. "The Faulty Logic of the Anti-Immigration Rhetoric." *NACLA* [North American Congress on Latin America] *Report on the Americas* 29, no. 3 (Nov./Dec. 1995): 18–23.

Muñoz, Cecilia. "Harassment in the Wake of Proposition 187." *Christian Science Monitor*, Dec. 27, 1994, p. 19.

Prince, Ron. "Americans Want Immigrants Out." *Los Angeles Times*, Sept. 6, 1994, p. B5.

"Proposition 187 and the Law of Unintended Consequences." *Los Angeles Times*, Oct. 2, 1994, p. M4.

Safire, William. "Self-Deportation?" *New York Times*, November 21, 1994, p. A15.

"Why Proposition 187 Won't Work." *New York Times*, Nov. 20, 1994, Sec. IV, p. 14.

Wilson, Pete. "California Won't Reward Lawbreakers." *Wall Street Journal*, Nov. 7, 1994, p. A14.

Ziv, Tal Ann, and Bernard Lo. "Denial of Care to Illegal Immigrants." *New England Journal of Medicine* 332, no. 16 (Apr. 20, 1995): 1095–1098.

Chapter 7: Immigration and Assimilation

Baron, Dennis. "English in a Multicultural America." *Social Policy* 21, no. 4 (Spring 1991): 5–14.

Chavez, Linda. *Out of the Barrio: Toward a New Politics of Hispanic Assimilation.* New York: Basic Books, 1991.

Crawford, James. *Hold Your Tongue: Bilingualism and the Politics of "English Only."* Reading, MA: Addison-Wesley, 1992.

Gallegos, Bee, ed. *English: Our Official Language?* New York: H.W. Wilson, 1994.

Hayakawa, S.I. "Bilingualism in America: English Should Be the Only Language." *USA Today* (Magazine), 118, no. 2530 (July 1989): 32–34.

Imhoff, Gary, and Gerda Bikales. "The Battle Over Preserving the English Language." *USA Today* (Magazine), 115, no. 2500 (Jan. 1987): 63–65.

Lang, Paul. *The English Language Debate: One Nation, One Language?* Springfield, NJ: Enslow Publishers, 1995.

Porter, Rosalie Pedalino. *Forked Tongue: The Politics of Bilingual Education.* New York: Basic Books, 1990.

Schlesinger, Arthur M., Jr. *The Disuniting of America.* New York: W. W. Norton, 1992.

Stalker, James C. "Official English or English Only." *English Journal* 77, no. 3 (Mar. 1988) 18–23.

Chapter 8: The Future of Immigration

Branigin, William. "Congress Finishes Major Legislation: Focus Is Borders, Not Benefits." *Washington Post*, October 1, 1996, pp. A1, A6.

_____. "Immigration Bill Attracts Broader Range of Opponents." *Washington Post*, September 28, 1996, p. A7.

Glazer, Nathan. "Immigration and the American Future." *Public Interest*, no. 118 (Winter 1995): 45–60.

Havemann, Judith, and Barbara Vobejda. "Advocacy Groups Across U.S. Preparing to Challenge Welfare Law." *Washington Post*, September 30, 1996, p. A8.

Heer, David M. *Immigration in America's Future: Social Science Findings and the Policy Debate.* Boulder, CO: Westview, 1996.

FURTHER READING

Andryszewski, Tricia. *Immigration: Newcomers and Their Impact on the United States.* Brookfield, CT: Millbrook, 1995

Bode, Janet. *New Kids in Town: Oral Histories of Immigrant Teens.* New York: Scholastic, 1991

Border Crossings: Emigration and Exile. Baltimore: Rosen, 1992

Burbur, William, ed. *Illegal Immigration,* "Current Controversies" series. San Diego: Greenhaven, 1994

Caroli, Betty L. *Immigrants Who Returned Home.* Broomall, PA: Chelsea House, 1990

Cockcroft, James D. *Latinos in the Making of the United States.* Danbury, CT: Franklin Watts, 1995

Cox, Vic. *The Challenge of Immigration.* Springfield, NJ: Enslow, 1995

Davies, Wendy. *Closing the Borders.* Austin, TX: Raintree Steck-Vaughn, 1995

Franklin, Paula A. *Melting Pot or Not? Debating Cultural Identity.* Springfield, NJ: Enslow, 1995

Harlan, Judith. *Bilingualism in the United States: Conflict and Controversy* Danbury, CT: Franklin Watts, 1995

Katz, William L. *The Great Migrations.* Austin,TX: Raintree Steck-Vaughn, 1993

Keene, Ann T. *Racism.* Austin, TX: Raintree Steck-Vaughn, 1995

Larking, Patricia. *Everything You Need to Know When a Parent Doesn't Speak English.* Baltimore: Rosen, 1994

Ocko, Stephanie. *Water: Almost Enough for Everyone.* New York: Atheneum, 1995

Press, Petra. *A Multicultural Portrait of Immigration.* Tarrytown, NY: Benchmark, 1996

Reimers, David M. *A Land of Immigrants.* Broomall, PA: Chelsea House, 1995

Szumski, Bonnie, ed. *Interracial America.* "Opposing Viewpoints" series. San Diego: Greenhaven, 1996

Takaki, Ronald. *From Exiles to Immigrants: The Refugees from Southeast Asia.* Broomall, PA; Chelsea House, 1995

Williamson, Chilton. *The Immigration Mystique: America's False Conscience.* New York: Basic, 1996

INDEX